SARAH PATTERSON

The
Distant
Summer

SIMON AND SCHUSTER·NEW YORK

FOR MY FATHER,
WHO'S HELPED ME ALL THE WAY

I was ever a fighter so—one fight more,
    the best and the last!
I would hate that Death bandaged my eyes
    and forbore
And bade me creep past.
                    —ROBERT BROWNING

PROLOGUE

I found my old diary yesterday. It was hidden between
the pages of a long-forgotten family Bible, and I was almost afraid to touch it. To read again a young girl's im-
pressions of first love. To remember his face and the calm
acceptance of death I had seen there. So I took it to the
terrace above the garden, where I could be alone to read
it in the half-light of dusk. To dream of such another evening, one distant summer, thirty years ago. . . .

1

IT WAS A WARM NIGHT. The last of the evening sun
filtered through the leaves of the beech trees, and
rooks called to each other across the branches. And into
this idyllic setting, a fugue in time, music floated. I followed the sound to the church in search of my father.

St. Peter's was his special joy, and the Norfolk flints in
its walls had seen the seasons turn for more than seven
hundred years. It was surprisingly large for such a tiny
village, but that was because of the prosperity the area
had enjoyed during the Middle Ages.

I followed the path through the churchyard between
the cypress trees and pushed open the great oak door of
the south porch. It was cool and dark inside, as it always
was. I stepped in and leaned against the doorpost, partly
to accustom my eyes to the light but also to listen to the
music for a while longer.

It was a beautiful performance, better than any I could
hope to give, sweet and clear. The sound of it seemed to
hang in the rafters, echoing and re-echoing faintly. I had
never heard anyone play like that before.

I slipped down the aisle and stood at the bottom of the

chancel steps by the pulpit. I couldn't see the organist, who was hidden by the green baize curtain, but a flying cap and tunic in RAF blue lay on the back of one of the choir stalls. There was a bomber station a couple of miles away across the fields. I presumed he must be from there, whoever he was—probably in search of solitude. He would scarcely be disturbed here in the evening. No one about but the odd woman from the village, praying for son or husband away at the war. For some reason I felt I was intruding, that I had no right to be there. I turned to go.

The music stopped, the last notes fading amongst the rafters, and sensing that the organist had moved, I turned again, curious. He was very young—certainly no more than eighteen or nineteen—and not very tall. But he had a pale, rather interesting face, and his hair was so fair as to be almost white. I hesitated, then went up the steps to the choir stalls.

"I'm sorry," I said. "I didn't mean to disturb you. I was looking for my father."

As I drew closer, a strange thing happened. The face was the same, yet not the same. There were lines there now, unperceived at a distance, cutting deeply into the forehead, tugging at the corners of the eyes, and the skin was stretched tight over the cheekbones.

He looked tired and drawn, like someone who had experienced too much in too little time, and what this boy had been through was engraved for all to see. It was the face of an old, old man, and something cold moved inside me.

"That's all right." He had a strangely dead voice. "I'm due out again soon, anyway. Must get back." He reached for his cap and tunic. "Who is your father?"

"The rector," I replied, mildly surprised because I had presumed he'd had permission to play.

"He hasn't been here while I've been playing."

I smiled. "But you wouldn't know if he had," I said. "You were lost in your music."

He grinned uncertainly, suddenly looking a lot younger.

"Do you play yourself?"

"Not like that. Not anything like that. I manage the hymns for Sunday service, but only because my father can't get anyone else. You know how it is. . . ."

"I know," he said, a sudden bitterness in his voice. "The war, the war, the bloody war. You'll have to excuse the language. It's a quotation. Some poet—I can't remember who." He stuck out a hand. "Johnny Stewart."

"Katherine Hamilton."

He held my hand for a moment. "What do you answer to? Kathie or Kate?"

"Either, I suppose."

"Kate." He nodded slowly, staring into space in an abstracted manner. "Yes, I like that. I shall call you Kate."

He pulled on his tunic. I was aware of the three stripes and crown of a flight sergeant on his sleeve, and above his left-hand tunic pocket the half-wing brevet of an air gunner with a single ribbon beneath it, alternating diagonal stripes of violet and white.

None of this meant very much to me. At that time there were so many aircraft in the skies above Norfolk that one rather took them for granted. American Flying Fortresses during the day, RAF Lancasters at night. In spite of all this, I knew very little about flying beyond what I read in the newspapers or heard on the radio.

Which, as I look back, was strange, for my father, as well as being rector of St. Peter's, was padre at the airfield with the rank of flight lieutenant in the RAF Volunteer Reserve. He looked well in uniform and wore wings himself and a row of medal ribbons, but they were from the

First World War, when he had been a pilot with the Royal Flying Corps.

When I was very young I remember him taking me to see a film called *Dawn Patrol* that was full of biplanes and dogfights and young men in open cockpits wearing leather helmets and goggles, white scarves blowing in the slipstream. The idea that my father, the man who ascended the pulpit in his vestments each Sunday to preach to his congregation, had ever been like that seemed utterly preposterous, and I dismissed the notion.

As Johnny Stewart buttoned his tunic I said, "So you're a flier?"

"More accurate to say I'm flown." He grinned. "I'm a rear gunner in a Lancaster bomber based at Upton Magna."

Upton Magna. How well I came to know that place. I have returned there only once since that distant summer. Four years ago, to see my mother, who was very ill. Dying, as it turned out.

It was the first week in November, late autumn, and the whole world seemed to be dying with her. It rained all the time I was there—a cold, unrelenting rain blowing in from the North Sea across the marshes. A sad, bleak autumnal world that exactly fitted my mood of quiet desperation, for to see one so greatly loved dying in great pain was hard to bear.

On the Friday morning of that terrible week I had walked out of the cottage into the rain, unable to bear the sight of her suffering for a moment longer. I didn't know where I was going and simply followed the field paths blindly, head down against the rain, my mother's old Labrador, Mister Jones, at my heels.

An hour must have passed, possibly more. I only know that I finally stopped under a tree to light a cigarette and when I looked up I could see the watch office and tower of Upton Magna airfield at the far end of the meadow. There was the rumble of an engine starting up.

I couldn't believe it. My stomach contracted and there was a sudden cold breath on my face. Was it then or now? I found myself running, Mister Jones at my heels, plowing through the long wet grass of the meadow.

I came out on a concrete runway and paused. It was cracked in a hundred places, infested with weeds. It was not the engine of a Lancaster I had heard starting into life, but a tractor moving towards a Forestry Commission wood on my right.

I remembered this place alive with activity, Lancasters waiting side by side at the dispersal points on quiet summer evenings. Ground crews swarming over them, preparing them for a raid that night, the roads busy with every kind of vehicle—trucks, cars, bicycles—and men on foot everywhere; so many young men.

Now only the main hangar was left, close to the watch office and water tower; the dispersal points were empty and the Nissen huts had disappeared, their foundations covered in grass.

The NCO's mess was still standing. I'd been in there more than once, but when I drew close I saw that the windows were shattered and most of the roof gone. I stood in the open doorway and looked across the piles of jumbled brick to the far wall. Depicted across the cracked plaster was a Lancaster dropping in for the kill—peeling now, faded by the years. It had been painted there in July, 1943, by Dad Walker, a flight sergeant navigator from Leeds killed over the Dutch coast on the twenty-second August of the same year on his forty-sixth op.

And in the corner there had been a piano. My eyes turned that way reluctantly. It had gone, of course, but for a moment I could hear voices and the same old songs echoed. "My Mother Comes from Norfolk"; "Take the Piston Rings out of My Stomach." And then it changed and there was only the piano—playing magnificently now, the sound of it filling my heart and mind with the marshes and the beauty of them, gulls flying in from the sea, the smell of wet earth, the incredible loneliness. . . .

So many young men. I walked to the door and stood staring out into the driving rain. Mister Jones, who had been waiting patiently, squatting on his haunches, stood up, legs braced, his entire body trembling, and started to whine. I leaned down to touch him. He whined again, turned and rushed off across the runway towards the village.

A flight of rooks lifted out of the trees nearby, calling harshly to each other as if disturbed by the dog's passing, and settled again. I was filled with a feeling of tremendous relief, as if a burden had been lifted from me; the earth moved, and I had to lean against the doorway for support.

I took a moment or so to pull myself together, then started off across the crumbling runway in Mister Jones's wake, half running. But when I got back to the cottage it was all over and my mother, God rest her, was dead.

Looking back to our first meeting that summer evening in the church, I found that he had actually told me very little about himself although we seemed to have talked for a long time. Presently he glanced at his watch and his eyes widened.

"I must go." He had risen as he spoke and he started up the aisle, putting on the cap as he went. He was almost out of the door when he turned as if on impulse and came back. "There's a dance in the village hall tomorrow. Like to come?"

I was two months away from my seventeenth birthday,

and except for the occasional church social I had never been to a dance in my life. Had never been allowed to go by my parents. Things were different then. Everything was different. I think he knew that I was going to stall, for the light died in his eyes; the face hardened, became old again. I seemed to see him shrink back inside the shell which had encased him when we first met.

So I surprised him and myself. "Yes," I said. "Thank you very much. I'd love to go." It was said, and my breath rushed out, because for some reason I'd held it in.

He smiled, and I was glad. "Where do I pick you up?"

"At the rectory. Ask anyone."

"At seven, then?"

"Yes."

He walked back up the aisle and out of the door. I felt strangely moved and quite breathless. Certainly I had no regrets about my decision, but would my parents? That was a bridge I would have to cross later. I pushed the thought of it firmly from my mind, went back to the organ and started to practice Sunday's hymns.

I arrived home to find my father already there, for the little Morris Eight saloon he used to get about the parish was parked in the drive. The lights were on in the front room. As I crossed the lawn my mother was drawing the heavy velvet curtains—rather belatedly considering the blackout regulations. When they had been pulled across, everything went quite dark, and I knew a moment of utter desolation and fear because I was so alone.

When I went in she was crossing the hall. "Hello," she said. "Where have you been?"

I took off my mac and followed her through to the kitchen. "I went up to the church to look for Daddy. There was a boy there playing the organ. I stayed to listen."

"What sort of boy?"

"From Upton Magna. A rear gunner."

"How old was he?" She was washing dishes now—always doing something.

"About nineteen, I think, but you should have seen his face. He was so tired, and he had lines on his forehead like—like an old man."

"Nice work they send young lads on nowadays." She was visibly moved and said a moment later, "Did he talk with you, then?"

"Yes."

"What about?" There was a certain edge to her voice, no more than that. I sought for the right words.

"Nothing very special. He needed someone to talk to and I was there. He asked me to the dance tomorrow."

"And what did you say?"

"I said yes."

"Even though we haven't met him yet?"

"He'll be picking me up here, so if you want to inspect him you can do it then."

"I see." She hesitated. "You're very young, Kathie. I wouldn't like . . ."

"For goodness' sake, Mummy," I said. "I'm just into the sixth form, and he's not long out of it from the looks of him." I suddenly felt terribly frustrated—frightened I suppose, that she wasn't going to understand; was going to get it all wrong. "He was just a lonely, quiet boy. He just wanted someone to talk to."

"We'll have to see what he's like, then, won't we? Your father's in the study. Tell him dinner's ready and wash your hands. I had to lay the table myself."

"I'm sorry."

She smiled suddenly and—unusual for her, for she kept her emotions on a tight rein—kissed me on the forehead. "Never mind, dear. It will all come out in the wash."

I thought of Johnny Stewart again, seemed to see that young, old man's face there in the half-light of the church, the bleak indifference in the empty eyes. I hugged her tightly, grateful for the love that kept me so secure and safe from harm here in this pleasant place.

"Katherine met a boy at the church this evening," said my mother carefully as she handed round the plates. "He was playing the organ."

My father removed his glasses from their case with care and put them on, his black eyebrows slightly raised. "Oh, yes?"

My mother carried on, "A rear gunner from Upton Magna."

I said quickly, "He asked me to the dance at the village hall and I accepted. He's picking me up here at seven to-morrow evening."

I always knew my father to be a remarkable man, but now he surprised my mother quite as much as me by simply saying calmly, "Will you walk or does he have a car? I must say these aircrew chaps seem to have access to un-limited supplies of petrol."

"I don't really know." I doubted very much that he owned a car.

"And he was hoping to collect you here?"

"Yes."

"Well, for the present I think we may say you can go," he said. "I presume we'll be allowed to meet him?"

"Yes. I'll invite him in."

"Good. Obviously your encounter was rather remarka-bly brief, but we must remember there's a war on." He smiled gently. "Did you find out his name, or wasn't there time enough for that?"

"Johnny," I said. "Johnny Stewart."

"And you said he is a rear gunner?"

"That's right."

"Poor lad."

He folded his hands together, bowed his head and began grace.

2

I WENT TO MY ROOM early that night. I didn't want to discuss Johnny any more. I didn't even want to think about him—just to be quiet for a while, to read a book and escape from my own thoughts. It didn't work, for in spite of myself I couldn't help wondering what he was doing at that precise moment. Again and again I found myself staring blankly at a page, deep in thought and, for some reason, choking a little when I swallowed.

The phone rang somewhere in another world and I surfaced from *Wuthering Heights*, a gloomy and depressing choice under the circumstances, and waited, half expecting that the call might be for me. When no one came, I put down the book and went out of the door.

As I walked along the landing, my father appeared from his room wearing his uniform. "There's a raid on?" I said quietly.

"Yes; your mother will be going up with me."

Two or three nights a week she worked for the WVS at Upton Magna. They had a caravan converted into a mobile canteen which dispensed coffee and tea to the aircrews going out on a raid or coming in from one.

"Where are they going this time?" I asked him.

"If I knew I wouldn't be allowed to tell you, now, would I?"

"No, of course not." I stood aside to let him pass and followed him down to the sitting room.

My mother was buttoning up the coat of her WVS uniform. "Don't wait up for me tonight," she said. "I'll probably not be home till breakfast. The kettle's just boiled, and there's tea made if you want some."

I kissed them both and they left quickly. I heard the engine of the Morris start up and fade away into the night. It seemed very quiet then. Too quiet, so I switched off the light and went to bed.

I heard the planes go out, rumbling overhead as usual. I lay for some time, listening and thinking about the men they carried, unwillingly reflecting on the fate of so many. Among them, someone I had just met who might not return at all.

My sleep was disturbed by bad dreams. Each time I wakened I could not remember what they had been, but the effect was such that in the end I was frightened to go back to sleep. It was the early hours of the morning—two o'clock, perhaps half-past. I heard a plane pass over very low and once again thought of Johnny Stewart.

My father's main problem when offered the living at Upton Magna had been my education. It was such an out-of-the-way little place, so much in the depths of rural Norfolk, that for a while it looked as if the only solution was boarding school, a fate I had managed to avoid until then. I'd been saved at the last moment by the happy chance that Cheriton, a girls' boarding school near Dover, had been evacuated to Tanbury House, a mile up the road from the village. My father had had words with Miss

Dean, the headmistress, who had agreed to take me as a day girl.

We had broken up for the summer holiday the previous week. I was to return reluctantly at the beginning of October to take Higher School Certificate, although my father had promised that I could join one of the services afterwards. For some reason my thoughts returned to one particular day in early June.

As usual, Miss Dean had taken assembly. It was a lovely morning. The sun shone in through the windows and the birds were singing. She read out the hymn number in a strangely distant voice and the piano broke into the opening chords of "Jerusalem." It is a beautiful hymn; the words and music convey such a poignant note of life that always when I hear it my heart lifts and I sing it loudly and clearly.

And so it was with every girl in the assembly that morning. The voices swelled up into the rafters. Miss Dean stood on the platform watching us silently, and slowly tears began to pour down her cheeks as we sang. She just stood there crying without making a noise.

The singers began to falter and one by one we stopped, and then the music teacher turned and saw us all standing there embarrassed and silent. Miss Dean walked down from the platform past all the teachers and into her study.

Afterwards, we learned that her brother, a submarine commander, had been posted as missing, presumed dead, in the North Atlantic.

At the time, Upton Magna had only been operating for three weeks, and some of the aircrew were billeted at the Grange, a mile away from the school. They used to cycle by in the late afternoons wearing flying kit. As they came down the road, they all rang their bells and blew their whistles. We would run to the windows to wave and shout, and they would call back as they swept on down the road, the sound fading in the summer heat.

We called them the Bicycle Boys. Had Johnny Stewart been one of them? Probably, and yet I had never noticed him and how could that be? How could I possibly have missed him? Now he was out there over Germany, but I pushed that thought firmly away from me and slept.

I woke again at dawn, drew back the curtain and stared into the cold morning. There was distant thunder on the horizon: the engines of the returning bombers. One by one, they swept in like gray ghosts, flying low as they came home.

I ran into the garden, my mac over my nightdress. The dew was wet to my bare feet, but I didn't mind the cold. Looking up as they passed overhead, I could see signs of fearful damage. One had part of its tail missing; another had holes in its wings.

And then I heard another engine coming in more slowly than the rest. It loomed out of the mist flying very low indeed. As it passed over I saw that half the starboard wing and one engine were missing, and most of the tail. There was smoke coming from the port outer engine, and the Lancaster was drifting down towards the hill now.

I saw a small black figure falling through air; a parachute opened, followed by another, and then the plane went in fast behind the trees. There was a tremendous explosion. The whole earth shook. I had a sickening feeling of utter horror, stood there staring at the black column of smoke rising into the sky beyond the hill, then turned and ran into the house.

I fell into an uneasy and troubled sleep after that. When I awakened it was just after nine. It was very quiet, only the rain tapping against the window. It was hard to believe that only a few hours earlier I had stood on the lawn in my bare feet and watched a plane plunge to its destruction, men die. Or perhaps it was just a dream after all? Perhaps it hadn't really happened. . . .

I dressed quickly and went downstairs. There was a note on the table. My mother had gone to the village stores; my father was at the church. I brushed my hair quickly, pulled on my old mac and went out.

My room had seemed quiet enough, but entering the church was like plunging into a deep pool. St. Peter's being Anglo-Catholic, there was a chapel to the Virgin Mary, and someone had lit a candle in front of her image. She seemed to be watching me, eyes turning as I went down the aisle to where my father knelt at the altar rail in prayer. I sat in the front pew and waited for him.

Finally he stood up and turned. He was still in uniform and badly needed a shave. "You slept late, Kathie."

"Yes."

There was only the silence again that always made me want to speak in a whisper. My throat was dry; the words didn't want to come and yet had to be said. "I saw the planes coming back at dawn. One of them crashed on the other side of the hill."

"Two of the crew got out—did you see that?"

"Yes."

"One broke his leg; the other is fine. I'm afraid the rest of them were killed." He added gently, "I checked on your friend, young Stewart. He's safe and well."

Relief swept over me like a wave. I closed my eyes for a moment, then turned and hurried out.

I heard a car enter the drive just before seven that evening, and as if by instinct I knew it was Johnny. I was almost afraid to see him and wondered if he had perhaps regretted the impulse that had made him ask me. I walked down the stairs very slowly and heard the sharp tap of the knocker against the front door.

"I'll answer it." My mother hurried along the hall, paused and then opened the door. Johnny stood on the doorstep. As he stepped inside I saw an old MG sports car parked at the bottom of the steps.

"You must be Sergeant Stewart," my mother said, closing the door.

"Yes. I'm supposed to be taking Kate to the dance at the village hall this evening."

She was surprised enough at the name to glance towards me, but said nothing. I stepped into the hall to meet him. He turned to face me and managed a slight smile.

"Hello," I said. "Let me take your coat."

"Thank you." He slipped his greatcoat off and handed it to me, and somehow I felt that this uniform helped the situation a little. My mother walked through into the sitting room, and Johnny stood back awkwardly for me to pass.

"This is Sergeant Stewart, Daddy," I said rather formally.

My father was sitting by the fire reading a book. He stood up carefully, laying the book aside, and shook hands. "Good evening, young man."

"Good evening, sir."

"You must be the organist."

Johnny glanced at me. "Yes, I suppose I am, sir."

For some reason I felt on the defensive. "The best I've ever heard."

"Which isn't saying a great deal," my father suggested gently.

It was the kind of remark he couldn't help making, a

product of that logical and precise mind of his; no malice intended at all.

There was a slight, awkward pause. Johnny said, "I'm sorry I didn't ask permission to play. There was no one around."

"That's all right. Feel free to go and play at St. Peter's anytime. It's a lovely old place. We're rather proud of it. Can I offer you a sherry?"

"Thank you very much, sir."

He was obviously being very careful, just like some sixth-former being entertained by the Head and making sure he doesn't put a foot wrong. My mother fetched glasses and the decanter. My father poured the sherry with infinite care, for it was hard to come by in those difficult days.

"My daughter seems to think you're good. Are you?"

It was as if they were playing some kind of game that had to be conducted according to their own rules. Johnny said calmly, "They let me into the Royal Academy of Music at fifteen. I won the Bach Award at the end of my first year, the Amersham Gold Medal for pianoforte during my second. And I was Gilson Organ Scholar." He sipped a little of his sherry. "Will that let me into the club, sir?"

There was a slightly mocking tone to his voice now, a kind of insolence. My father chose to ignore it. "And then you joined up?"

"That's it."

"Satisfied, Daddy?" I demanded.

My father took no notice. "There's a Bechstein grand in the conservatory that gets little use these days. You're welcome anytime."

My mother said, "Get the tea, dear; the kettle should be boiled by now."

I went into the kitchen and busied myself with the

tray. There was a step behind. When I turned I found that my father had followed me. I could hear my mother chatting brightly to Johnny in the sitting room.

He started to fill his pipe. "A nice boy. Brave, too, from the looks of things."

I paused, the kettle in my hand. "What makes you say that?"

"That ribbon he's wearing; it's the DFM."

I was incredibly ignorant about that kind of thing in spite of the fact that there was a war on. I said, "What's that?"

"The Distinguished Flying Medal. Here, I'll show you."

He opened a cupboard, rummaged amongst the old newspapers stacked inside and produced a copy of the *London Illustrated News,* several months old. In those days it used to be filled with features on the services, and he opened it at a section headed AWARDS FOR GALLANTRY. There were facsimiles of fifteen or twenty medals with their ribbons, all reproduced in color.

The first thing I noticed was a ribbon my father wore. White, purple and white—the Military Cross. Underneath it said various things about heroism and gallantry. I looked at him blankly. "But you've got this one."

"That's right. In the old Flying Corps days it was military decorations they handed out." I wanted an explanation and got none. "It's the RAF section you want—here."

Distinguished Service Order, Distinguished Flying Cross—they were for officers. For NCOs, the Distinguished Flying Medal and the Conspicuous Gallantry Medal.

I read what it said underneath about bravery and courage in the face of the enemy, but none of it seemed to have anything to do with Johnny any more than the other had with my father.

I said, "But why do they have different medals for

officers? It's the same war, isn't it? They're flying the same planes?"

"Good old British class distinction, I'm afraid." He smiled wryly. "Just the same in the other services, but for some reason it's particularly noticeable in the RAF. A pilot, for instance, stands a far better chance of picking up a DFC if he's an officer than he does of getting his DFM if he's an NCO. I'm not saying a lot of DFCs aren't well and truly earned, but a large number do seem to be awarded for simply completing a tour or something like that." He put a match to his pipe. "Come to think of it, the highest-scoring pilot in the Battle of Britain was a flight sergeant, and yet many officer pilots who had shot down fewer enemy planes received more decorations than he did."

"I think that's shocking."

"Which all means," he said, "that when you see a DFM ribbon on display, you can be pretty certain it's been awarded for an act of real bravery in genuinely shaky conditions." He picked up the tray. "Yes, as I said, a brave boy. Shall we go in?"

"Is your father in the RAF, Johnny?" my mother said.

He was standing with his back to the fire, his sherry on the mantelpiece. He said, "No, he's a lieutenant colonel in the Royal Engineers. Last heard of with the Eighth Army in North Africa or wherever they are these days. A regular soldier."

"Presumably he'd have preferred you to join the Army?" my father said.

Johnny nodded. "Quite true, sir, but I wanted to fly."

I sensed a barrier there, but my mother carried on, "And your mother?"

He sipped a little of his sherry, taking his time, then said calmly, "Dead, Mrs. Hamilton. Four years ago."

"I'm sorry."

"Don't be. It was the best thing for her in the circumstances."

There was a silence. My mother said hesitantly, "Do you have any brothers or sisters?"

"None. An aunt and uncle in Aberdeen, the Scottish side of things. There are my father's relatives, but I haven't seen anything of them in several years now." He put down his cup. "I'll try that Bechstein now, if I may."

My father led the way into the conservatory. The Bechstein stood beside French windows which opened to a terrace above the garden at the rear of the house. I played it a little myself, of course, but my father was right. It needed using.

Johnny sat down on the plush seat of the old Victorian stool and lifted the lid from the keys. He stayed there for a moment, flexing his hands, then started to play "Pavane for a Dead Infanta." It would have wrung tears from a stone on the shore. He made it sound the most hauntingly beautiful piece I'd ever heard in my life. By any standards he was quite brilliant.

My mother sat with her eyes closed, raptly drinking in the music. As for my father—his face was quite white, and I don't think I've ever seen him so astonished, so impressed. My throat went dry, my heart ached and I went to the piano and stood at Johnny's side. When he finished, he went straight into a Bach prelude, a crisp, ice-cold, precise piece that had to be played very fast. Halfway through, he stopped abruptly. I noticed that he gripped his left arm tightly and noticed something else, too. The skin on the back of his hands was stretched tight and very shiny.

My father said, "You'll carry on after the war, I presume?"

"The piano?" Johnny shook his head and held out his

hands. "They aren't quite what they were. I was in a fire last year, and I got shrapnel in my left arm. It tires easily. I'd never get through a piano concerto." All this was delivered in the calmest of voices. "I amuse myself with a little composing, but it's all the same in the end, if you think about it."

My father's face was paler than ever now. He said, "Yes, I see what you mean."

Johnny stood up and turned to me. "Better be off, Kate, if you're fit."

"I'll get your coat, dear," my mother said.

We went out into the hall and my father opened the door. "Those French windows out there are never kept locked, Johnny. You can come and go as you like. I'd take it as a favor."

"That's very kind of you, sir." Johnny smiled. "I might just take you up on that."

He took me by the arm and we went down the steps to the MG.

3

T HE MG HAD SEEN considerable service. The door was wired into place, so that I had to climb over rather inelegantly to reach my seat. But once you were inside, the car seemed to hold you fast in its hand.

"You don't need the hood up, do you?"

"No, this is fine."

He let in the clutch and drove away.

By that stage in the war private motoring no longer existed, although people like my father got a ration of two or three gallons a week for essential purposes. They used to say that if you saw a private car on the road, it was being driven by either a doctor, a minister or a member of the WVS motor pool which existed in most country areas to help in emergencies.

I said, "How do you manage for petrol for this thing?"

"No trouble," he said. "Anything goes for our gallant boys in blue. Even bacon and eggs for breakfast. Didn't you know that?"

There was a hard, cynical edge to his voice that I didn't like, but I wasn't going to allow anything to spoil this. The MG rattled alarmingly. The state it was in, I don't think he ever once managed to get the needle past the forty mark, and yet the sensation of speed was incredible.

We went round the bend in the road below the rectory and the wind caught my hair, whipping it up and back from my face. It was marvelous; wonderful to lie there as we hurtled through the quiet evening along the green tunnel of the road, the branches of the trees joining overhead. I turned to look at him and found him trying to shake a cigarette out of a packet of Players.

"Let me." I found that I had to shout above the noise of the engine.

I put the cigarette in my mouth to light it for him and leaned over out of the wind, striking a match. I'd seen Claudette Colbert do this for Ronald Colman in a film and had been much impressed. All I succeeded in doing now was burning my fingers and taking in a lungful of smoke that almost finished me off.

I leaned back, coughing. Johnny took the cigarette from between my fingers. "You'll stunt your growth and take ten years off your life. Better not to start."

"What about you?" I demanded.

"Ah, well, in my case it doesn't make much difference."

That remark honestly didn't mean anything to me. That was to come later. One of the side straps had worked loose on the bonnet, and he pulled in at the side of the road to fasten it.

It was very quiet. For some reason I said, "I saw the plane crash this morning."

"Did you?"

"Those poor men. Were any of them friends of yours?"

"I knew two of them. I'd just seen the others around." He seemed completely disinterested.

I couldn't understand his attitude. He had seemed such a sensitive person. I said indignantly, "How can you be so callous when two of your friends were burnt to death this morning?"

"It's easy enough when you've seen as many die as I have."

That shut me up. Here was something I couldn't quite touch on—a cold indifference that was somehow terrifying. He buckled the strap and looked out through the trees across the salt marsh. The sky was dark now along the line of the horizon.

"It's a godforsaken sort of place."

"Oh, you'd be surprised," I said. "Most people in the village actually go to church. Don't you?"

He had clambered back behind the wheel and turned to look at me in genuine surprise. "You must be joking."

He drove away quickly and I leaned back against the seat, pushing the implications of everything he had said away from me. Just now I was only concerned with the sheer bliss of being there with him. The flying cap was tilted down across his forehead, that pale, almost white hair blowing in the wind. He had the collar of his greatcoat turned up and sat there, another cigarette jutting from one corner of his mouth, hand steady on the wheel. I couldn't believe this was happening, and my skin seemed to prickle with delight.

The ladies' cloakroom at the village hall was quite inadequate for such an event and was hopelessly crowded. There were one or two girls from local farms that I knew who looked my way in astonishment, obviously surprised to see me there. The rest were all strangers. Land girls from the surrounding villages and quite a few WAAFs from Upton Magna.

I got rid of my coat and managed to find space in front of a mirror for a second. I was wearing an old white school blouse and a little black velvet bow tie to match the black velvet skirt which my mother had run up from a prewar evening skirt. She had also lent me a pair of silk stockings—heavily darned, but not where it showed. Something else in distinctly short supply at that time.

I wasn't wearing makeup at all, didn't really need any with these heavy, dark eyebrows of mine and the long lashes which I'd always thought of as a curse. I tried a little lipstick and stood back to get a better view. It could have been worse, very definitely, and then someone elbowed me out of the way. For some reason, I was shaking like a leaf. I took a deep breath, opened the door and went out.

Johnny was leaning against the wall, smoking another of those eternal cigarettes of his, watching the crowd, and there was that bleak, lonely look on his face again. It was as if he didn't belong; on the outside looking in.

I stood beside him and took his hand. "Penny for them?"

He came back to life with a start and focused on me. His face broke into a slow smile. "You look marvelous."

"Oh, that's just the low lights," I said, my face hot.

"Is it true you're not seventeen yet? Your mother made quite a point of that."

"She would."

"And they'd like you home by ten-thirty."

I could have exploded with rage and then saw his mouth quiver at the corner. As he started to laugh I found myself laughing with him.

He put an arm about my shoulders. "We'd better get some dancing in, then, hadn't we?"

The hall was packed with uniforms, men laughing, drinking, forgetting. There was a three-piece band on the platform—piano, double bass and drums. The pianist and bass player were RAF boys, both flight sergeants, but the drummer was something of a surprise. He wore an American uniform—a captain, although I didn't know that until later. He had red hair cropped very short—almost a crew cut, but not quite—and a handsome, reckless face, a slight fixed smile on his mouth.

He was a tremendously attractive person, full of vitality and gaiety, and he never stopped looking about him as if perpetually searching for something. It was only on closer inspection that I saw that his eyes weren't smiling. Just like Johnny.

There was another extraordinary thing about him. He had the silver wings of a pilot above the left breast pocket, and one of the medal ribbons he wore there was a British DFC. I knew that from the article in the *London Illustrated*, the only difference being the little silver rose on the ribbon. Above his right-hand pocket were RAF pilot's wings.

He glanced our way casually, then looked back, eyes widening in surprise. "Hey, Johnny!" he called. "What's new?"

His drumming didn't falter. Johnny waved. "Keep trying, Richie! You might make it yet."

The American grinned and we moved away into the crowd, circling the floor. "A friend of yours?" I asked.

"Richie?" Johnny gave a funny little half-smile. "Bound together by blood, guts and piano wire." I was bewildered and it showed. "Sorry—a favorite phrase of his. I did my first tour with Richie. We were on Halifaxes then."

"But he's an American," I said.

"Oh, a lot of their boys joined the RAF before America came into the war. Most of them were in the Eagle Squadron flying Spitfires, but a few found their way into bombers."

I remembered vaguely having read about it some-where. "But didn't they wear RAF uniforms?"

"That's right, with a special patch on the left shoulder to show they were Yanks. They were all transferred into the United States Army Air Forces last September."

"And Richie?"

"He'd been with us so long he didn't take kindly to the idea of changing uniform. Managed to avoid it until last month; then they made it official in spite of him."

"So what's he doing here?"

"He was into his third tour. Twenty operations to go. They didn't want to disturb his crew, so he stays on by special arrangement until he reaches his ninetieth. Then it's back to good old Uncle Sam whether he likes it or not."

I frowned. "His ninetieth? That seems rather a lot."

He said carelessly, "Oh, Richie is hot stuff. A real ace. DSO, DFC and bar and the Legion of Honor for some nonsense or other he got into with a Free French squad-ron. If he was back with his own people he'd probably be one of these twenty-three-year-old lieutenant colonels the Yanks are so fond of."

"Don't you like Americans?"

He frowned in bewilderment. "Like them? Good God, if the rest are anything like Richie, I love 'em all."

The trio came to the end of the number they were play-ing and eased into "A Foggy Day in London Town." Johnny took my hand and threaded his way through the crowd to the stand.

"I'll spell you for a while, Bunny," he said.

The pianist, a flight sergeant pilot who looked even younger than Johnny, got up from his seat still playing, and Johnny sat down and took over.

Richie said, "What's this, Johnny, women at your age? Whiskey and cards next."

"You go to hell, Yank," Johnny said amiably. "This is Kate Hamilton and you'd better be polite. Her father is padre at the base."

"The guy with the pilot's wings?" Richie said, not in the least put out. "I used to run for cover every time I saw him; then somebody told me he was flying Camels on the western front in 1917, just like my old man. I'd love to talk to him."

"That's easy enough to arrange. Come to tea on Sunday," I said.

He bowed from the waist, still drumming. "A shame to see a nice girl like you in bad company."

"Notice the manners," Johnny put in. "Very Old World. Richie, I should tell you, is what is known as a Creole. New Orleans French. His great grandfather used to shoot men under the elms at dawn if they displeased him."

"Those were the days," Richie said, "and the name, by the way, is Richaud. Flight Lieutenant—sorry; force of habit, that—*Captain* Henri Richaud, USAAF, and don't let the boy wonder here throw you. He's been around so long he thinks he can walk on water."

"Shut up and play," Johnny told him.

And they were good. Richie could do more than just tap that drum in time, and Johnny was tremendous, playing with a solid driving force. "A Foggy Day," "American Patrol," "G.I. Jive." In a matter of minutes the whole place seemed to really come alive.

After that he just kept on playing, and it was Richie who passed the drumsticks over to a young pilot officer half an hour later and led me down to the dance floor.

"You won't get any more out of him tonight. His one and only love, the piano."

We circled the floor. The lights were very low now, the

air full of cigarette smoke. He held me close and yet I didn't feel in the slightest that he was making a pass.

"You're good," he said.

"Ballroom dancing twice a week at my school. Tuesdays and Fridays instead of hockey if you wanted. They were very progressive."

"Don't tell me," he said. "Let me guess. You girls always had to dance together. Not a boy in sight."

"It was that kind of school."

"Was or is? How old are you, anyway?"

"Sixteen," I told him. "Seventeen on the twentieth of August. Leo. We can be very difficult."

"My God." He eased away. "It's like the song says. They're either too young or too old. Where did you meet Johnny?"

"In church. He was playing the organ."

"Well, that figures." He shook his head. "What a war."

"Johnny told me you flew together. Halifaxes, he said."

"That's right. Our first tour. You want to hear a funny story? The first time we met I found him in my kite looking it over. They'd just been showing a party of air-training cadets around the base. You know—schoolboys. Johnny looked so young I thought he was one of them. Told him to get the hell out of it." He shook his head. "He was just eighteen and looked two years younger."

"And after that you became friends?"

"Friends?" Something clicked in his eyes and he was suddenly serious. "Friends? Oh, yes, I think you could say that. We've got one big thing in common, Johnny and me. We're still around." The music stopped. He stood there for a moment holding my hand. "That's important because in our business it's almost unique."

"I see," I said, and there was a coldness inside me. A kind of fear, I suppose.

He nodded slowly. "You know something? I think you

could be just the thing for the boy wonder. Maybe you can keep him walking on water. Not so good for you, mind."

"Why do you call him that? The boy wonder."

"A joke," he said. "A bad, bad joke."

The music started again and he smiled. "And now I think I'll take you back while those good old finer instincts are still operating."

Johnny gave the piano back to the boy called Bunny for a while and danced with me. I said, "Richie is quite a character."

"Oh, don't be deceived by all that surface charm," he said. "Underneath he's still a sensitive soul."

"Can you prove that?"

"Easy. He flies a rather distinctive Lanc with a very large Stars and Stripes painted on the side. *J for Jenny* it used to be called. After a rather snotty young deb he met in the downstairs bar at the Ritz and fell in love with."

"Used to be called?"

"She married a major in the Grenadiers. An earl, if you please. Richie had the name of his Lanc changed to *Jenny Gone*. Is that sensitive enough for you?"

It made me cringe, go cold inside. What kind of world had I walked into? What kind of men were these? I'd never been out with a boy in my life. I know that may sound unbelievable now, but in those days it was common enough for a girl of my age. Yet there I was, dancing with a stranger, no more than a couple of years older than me on paper, a thousand in terms of experience of life. A boy barely out of school. At another time, he would very probably have been in his first year at university. Instead, he was old beyond his years; ground down by a nightmare of violence, destruction; death a daily occurrence. Even Richie, who, as I was to discover later, was looked upon as an old man, was only twenty-three years of age.

I suppose this all sounds very melodramatic, but you must understand that that was exactly how I felt, then, at that particular moment of time in the summer of 1943, and it is all precisely recorded in my diary.

Richie was at the punch a great deal after that, and I also saw him drink from a flask he carried in his hip pocket. Not that he seemed drunk, but when we left at ten-fifteen he squeezed himself into the space behind the two front seats of the MG, his legs dangling over the boot, and went to sleep. When we turned into the drive and halted at the front door, a chink of light showed through the living-room curtains.

Johnny said, "Thanks—I enjoyed it."

He didn't even kiss me on the cheek and somehow it didn't matter. You see, the whole thing had seemed so different, so important in itself, that that was enough. It struck me suddenly, and not without a certain wry humor, that if I'd been back at school and had described the evening to any of my friends, not one of them would have believed me.

"She's a great little dancer," Richie said, his voice muffled. "You should try her sometime."

Johnny ignored him. "That offer your father made for me to use the piano—was he serious?"

"You heard what he said. Come and go as you please. The French windows are never locked."

"Good, then I'll be along tomorrow. I don't think it's likely we'll have anything on. Probably in the morning. See you then."

It was a statement, not a request, and the heart moved inside me. I got out of the MG as gracefully as I could considering it was necessary for me to scramble over the wired-up door.

"I'd think about it if I were you," Richie said in that muffled voice. "After all, what about me? What about that special relationship between our two great countries?"

Johnny reached over and rammed Richie's cap over his eyes. "Tomorrow," he said, and drove away.

I don't think I've ever known such a feeling of pure excitement, of just being alive, as I felt at that moment, standing there at the bottom of the steps, listening to the noise of the MG fade into the night.

4

I WOKE EARLY NEXT MORNING in spite of the fact that I'd
been late to bed. I lay there for quite a while listening
to the quiet. I could hear my heart beating, and my stomach ached with an ache that had nothing to do with hun-
ger for food.

I got up; dressed in old jodhpurs, sweater and riding
boots and crept downstairs. I could hear the clatter of a
pan on the stove in the kitchen, where my mother was
preparing breakfast, but tiptoed past and let myself out of
the front door.

I needed action and sought it in the usual way. There
was a farm a few hundred yards up the lane from the rectory. A small holding owned by a nice old man called
Hervey. With a son and daughter away at the war, he and
his wife ran the place between them. One thing they
couldn't cope with was a three-year-old hunter named
Jersey Lil, which was where I came in. I gave Lil an hour
or two most days, as much for myself as for her.

Ten minutes later I was galloping across the top
meadow, head down against the rain; I jumped the fence
at the far end and turned into a bridle path through trees.

When I came out on the edges of the marsh I dropped into a canter and finally halted. Lil was blowing gently, sides heaving, and put her head down to eat.

I had, until that moment, managed to keep any thoughts of Johnny Stewart outside the circle of my consciousness, although the ache had moved up from stomach to brain as if to indicate that something was knocking persistently on the door and would not be denied.

There was a dull rumble as of thunder, north by northwest. A squadron of Flying Fortresses moved across the sky, still climbing, turning out to sea, headed for Holland. I sat staring up at them, watching the vapor trails. There were men up there, some of them just boys like Johnny. I was safe and secure in an English meadow, and they were headed towards death and destruction over Germany within a matter of hours. Many of them wouldn't be flying back, because at that time American losses in daylight bombing raids over Germany were really dreadful. Even those who came back would carry their quota of dead and dying with them. . . .

And Johnny was just like them. He was a night bird—the only difference. Death and destruction, violence and killing, sitting behind his machine guns, watching, waiting. How strange that someone so sensitive, so talented, should come to that. The thought was more than I could bear, and I turned Lil away from the marsh, put my heels to her and galloped back towards the farm.

As I walked up the drive I could hear the piano. It was still raining, but in spite of that, when I went round to the conservatory terrace, the French windows stood open.

Johnny was seated at the Bechstein wearing a white polo-necked sweater, his tunic unbuttoned. He was smoking. In fact, when I picture him in my mind's eye as he was at that time, there is always a cigarette jutting from

one corner of his mouth. He glanced up, smiled very
slightly, but said nothing. I sat down in one of the old
easy chairs by the empty fireplace and listened and
watched.

A great many of the things he played I knew, and it
was a strange enough mixture. Some jazz; a snatch or two
of boogie-woogie, very popular at that time; a number of
popular standards, the kind of thing he had played at the
dance; with some Chopin and Bach and Mozart thrown
in to stiffen the mixture.

And he was good. Everything he played, each in its
separate way, was first-rate, and he played with a kind of
physical intensity that was rather moving. He *became* the
music somehow, so that there was an emotional quality to
it, a feel that was something very special. But then, I was
already prejudiced.

My mother entered, balancing a tea tray in one hand
and holding the door open with the other so that it didn't
bang and disturb him. She put the tray down carefully;
nodded to me, a finger to her lips, and crept out. He must
surely have been aware of her presence, yet gave no sign,
so involved did he seem to be in his playing.

And then he moved into something else, something I
had never heard before. It was strangely sad and forlorn.
I have since come across a word that describes it perfectly. *Dreichness*—a Gaelic term, I believe, that stands
for the terrible despairing sadness that is in the heart of a
brave man standing on the edge of night who knows that
there is nothing and nothing and yet nothing. . . .

All this was in the music, and yet in the despair was
strength, a strange kind of life, all its own, which en-
veloped me and drew me in. At first I wanted to cry, but
that feeling soon passed, for what I was listening to now
was too important for such a trivial response.

The music tailed away, then stopped. He slammed

down the lid of the Bechstein in anger and I sensed a great frustration.

"What was that?" I asked.

"Something I'm trying to put together. A kind of tone poem for the piano. I seem to have lost it somehow. I get it to that point, then can't go on. It's lacking something, God knows what, but it is."

"But it's marvelous," I said. "Truly it is." I poured the tea. "You said it was a tone poem. What about?"

"Oh, the marshes, the birds, those vast shorelines out there." He got up and walked to the French windows. "I'd like to catch it all, get it down while . . ." He hesitated.

While there's still time. I knew that was what he had been about to say. I handed him his tea. "Norfolk, you mean? I think that's a wonderful idea. The most rural county still left in the country. Daddy says it's much the same as it was in Victorian times in most of the villages, except for some of the modern machinery you see about, and there isn't much of that on some farms."

"And the bombers," he said. "Overhead, night and day. Don't forget them."

"Two-way traffic," I said brightly.

"Only for some, Kate," he said somberly. He frowned. "You've been riding."

"I'm glad you've noticed me at last."

He was immediately contrite. "Sorry. I'm not in the best of moods this morning."

"You need some air. A change of scene. We'll go for a walk on the marsh. You can borrow a pair of Daddy's Wellingtons." He appeared to hesitate, and I added, "Who knows—you might get some inspiration." My voice dwindled. I wasn't really very sure of myself.

As I wrote in my diary later, he made an effort that was very obviously for my sake. "Yes, that would be fine." His mouth twisted into that ready smile that was always missing from the eyes. "Just the thing to blow the cobwebs away."

Most of the desolate marsh was underwater when the tide came in, but that wouldn't be until early evening. The channel of the creek was clearly defined, and beyond it there was a wide expanse of mud flats, dikes rising above in green lines. There were birds in the great banks of reeds. Grebes, moorhens, curlew, widgeon, brent geese and gulls of every shape and variety, swooping in above the sand dunes on the far side of the marsh, the gray North Sea beyond.

We walked across, following one of the dike paths, birds scattering angrily out of the reeds on either side as we approached. It was still raining, and Johnny wore an old trench coat of my father's. Presently, we came out near the end of the beach at the Point and started across the mud flats towards the dunes. A bird rose from a clump of reeds in alarm, breaking into a loud, musical bubbling song.

"A curlew," I said. "Earlier than usual. They don't arrive much before autumn generally."

Johnny stood quite still, hands thrust deep into the pockets of the trench coat, watching it circle into the rain and fly away. "I'd like to catch that sound. It somehow sums the whole thing up. Everything I'm trying to say."

We carried on walking. "What do you usually do—for a piano, I mean?" I asked him.

"There's an old upright in the NCOs' mess. Not much, but better than nothing. It's difficult because there's nearly always someone in there. But I manage."

"And that's why you tried the organ at the church?"

"That was just chance. I was out for a walk and decided to have a look inside. Most church organists tend to keep their instruments locked. I've never been across here before. I always thought it would be too dicey."

"It can be," I said. "Come across at the wrong time and there's nowhere more dangerous. I'll show you the wrecks sometime when the tide is right. People have just disappeared without a trace."

"Some kind of local bogeyman?" he said, for I think he was inclined to disbelieve me.

"The only bogeyman around here is the sea."

"Why don't they run for it?"

"They haven't a chance. It creeps up on you like . . . like some living thing and swamps the whole of the mud flats within half an hour when it's really moving. You have to know what you're doing. We could go right across one day, but for the moment, I think we'll just aim for the sand dunes."

There was a sort of personality change in him then. He seemed happier than I had known him, suddenly cheerful, throwing jokes at me one after the other. We even had a race when we reached the great shingle bank above the sea.

"No mines?" he asked.

I shook my head. "No need. It's dangerous enough."

He threw stones into the waves, smiling all the time. I think he had forgotten flying. I suspect he had even forgotten his music for the time being. He just walked along at my side, smiling constantly at something I said or perhaps at his own thoughts. He was so relaxed that he didn't even light a cigarette.

"Where's your home?" I asked him.

"Wherever I'm posted. Used to be in Yorkshire. A village not too far from York. That's where I first went to school. We used to have horses. You'd have liked it."

"Yes, I like to ride," I said. "My favorite way of blowing away those cobwebs you mentioned. A good, fast gallop with the rain in your face."

"My father hunts when he's home." There was a trace of bitterness there. "I used to ride myself. I had a chestnut stallion. A six-year-old. I kept him in stables for a while. Sold him before I came up here. My mother gave him to me, you see, so he was completely mine. I can't see *your* father riding, somehow."

"He's very resourceful and very brave," I said. "He must be, because he was flying fighter planes in the First World War when he was only your age. But riding—that would be something else again. He's tried, but once up there he just goes rigid."

"You're lucky to have someone like that. He's a fine man."

"I think so." We walked on in silence, for we had obviously touched on areas that were painful for him. "I don't really know all that much about you," I said, "and you know everything about me."

"That's because your life is so uncomplicated. Too young to join one of the services, and you've never been away from home—except to school, and that doesn't really count."

"No adventures at all."

"No calamities either. The sweet life."

A rabbit ran along the grass at the edge of the shingle. "Look," I said, and slipped, rattling some stones.

It ran for its burrow, the gray-white bobbing tail the last we saw of it. Johnny was laughing, looking very young, very natural; and then I heard the drone of an engine. He turned quickly to look out to sea. A Flying Fortress was coming in towards the coast trailing smoke from one engine. It was dropping lower and lower. Something was very wrong.

"Come on, come on, get her out of it!" That was

Johnny. His fists were clenched and he glared up into the sky as the great bomber passed, very low now. I think he was willing it to rise, and for a while it looked as if the pilot was succeeding. "That's right!" he called. "Pull her up! Steady, for God's sake!"

His voice was raised to a shout, his face straining with effort. "Get her up!" His last shout trailed away into a groan as the Fortress swooped down in the far distance. There was silence, then a dull, muffled explosion. A black column of smoke spiraled into the air three or four miles away.

He stood very still, fists clenched. Then he fished in his tunic pocket for a cigarette and stuck it in his mouth. He put a match to it and inhaled deeply. When he turned, the eyes were bleak again, the face calm.

"We'd better get back."

"Johnny?" I put a hand on his arm.

"Don't say it, Kate. Let's just get moving."

I realized suddenly, or perhaps the realization came later, that any attempt at consolation would only have made him angry. It wasn't really grief he felt, in any case. I think he *was* angry. Angry at the waste.

He didn't say another word, simply walked back very fast so that I had to half-run to keep up with him. My mind was a turmoil. Conflicting emotions. I wanted to help, wanted to say the right thing, but what *was* the right thing to say? What did I have that could possibly ease that terrible pain?

When we reached the rectory it was raining quite hard, and we ran the last hundred yards, straight up the steps and into the hall. I took off my coat. When I turned he was pulling off the Wellington boots.

"Thank your father for the loan. I'll be off now."

"Don't be silly," I said. "We'll be having lunch soon."

I walked into the conservatory without waiting for a reply, because it seemed the most natural place to go, and he followed me. I stood beside the Bechstein and put a hand on it. "There's still this."

"How long for?" he said gravely.

"Does it matter? All we ever have is a day at a time."

He burst into astonished laughter and put his hands on my shoulders. "Where in the hell do you get all this deepseated wisdom from, anyway?"

I had the grace to look slightly shamefaced. "That bit was from my father's sermon last Sunday."

He brushed his knuckles across my chin. "You're marvelous, do you know that, Kate? The best there is." He turned to sit down at the piano. Thank God he did, for my face was suddenly hot and I had difficulty in holding back the tears. "You're right," he said. "I've still got my music and the will to do it, if only it would come out right."

"Don't try too hard. Let it take time to form in your mind and work at it slowly. Take it as it comes and it *will* come, I'm sure of it."

He started to play—his own music, the piece he had been working on—and now I recognized it for what it was. The marsh, the birds, the sea and the infinite loneliness. He even had the curlew in there, calling plaintively.

He played on with exquisite delicacy and feeling, looked up and smiled. "I think I know what's missing, but I'm not sure of it—how to grasp it and keep it fast, put it into the music. I'm not sure of myself, that's the trouble. Who *am* I, Kate? What in the hell is it all about? Could I be dreaming, do you think?"

I didn't understand, didn't comprehend for one moment what he was trying to say. But he was talking, wasn't he? And playing? The link with life was enough for the present.

There was a roar of an engine in the lane outside; tires skidded to a halt in the gravel at the front door. "What's that?" I said.

Johnny went out through the French windows. I hurried after him. Richie was sitting astride a motorbike at the bottom of the steps. He wore his peaked cap, flying jacket and boots, and his face was pale with excitement.

"What's up?" Johnny demanded.

"Big flap on," Richie said. "Daylight raid on Kiel. One of these in-and-out jobs. Group have asked for six planes. I'm leading."

"What about my lot?"

"Not this time, but I'm short of a mid-upper gunner. Jack Thompson's gone down with flu."

He didn't ask Johnny to go, and there certainly wasn't any question of ordering him, for as I learned later, he didn't have the right. He just sat there, waiting.

"Johnny?" I put a hand on his sleeve.

He turned, his face very pale, the mouth twisted in an ugly, cynical smile. "See what I mean? Find someone with a future, Kate, and forget me. I'm already dead."

I think it was the most terrible thing I'd ever heard anyone say in my life. I tried to reply, but the words wouldn't come. Johnny flung a leg over the pillion seat, and Richie turned to look at me, his face working. It was as if he were trying to say something, but then there simply wasn't the time. He opened the throttle, the rear wheel skidded and they were down the drive and into the lane in a moment, the noise fast dwindling into the distance.

When I turned, the door was open and my father stood there. I knew by the expression of deep pain on his face that he must have been there long enough to hear the important bit. "Kathie?" he said, and put out a hand.

A curlew cried high in the rain, swooping in across the

beech trees—perhaps the one we had seen down there on the marsh, come to mock me.

I picked up a stone and threw it up into the air. "Damn you!" I cried. "Damn you and damn you and damn you!"

I turned; ran up the steps, eluding my father's outstretched hand, and went up to my room.

I spent a restless afternoon, constantly watching from my window for any sign of the returning Lancasters. I was in the garden just before evening, cutting roses for my mother, when I heard the engines. I dropped basket and scissors and hurried up to the terrace, where I had laid my father's Zeiss field glasses ready on the balustrade.

When I focused them, the lead plane jumped clearly into view. There was the picture of an exotic-looking girl painted just beneath the cockpit and the legend *Rita Hayworth*. I turned to the second and then the third. There were five in all, no apparent damage, but *Jenny Gone* wasn't amongst them.

I waited, hoping that it was just later back than the others. A quarter of an hour went by, but there was no sound from the horizon. It had stopped raining long since; the evening sky was very blue, very empty. There was a step behind me and my father moved out on the terrace.

"Anything?" he asked.

Before I could reply there was a sudden distant buzz. He moved beside me, took the glasses and raised them to his eyes. He lowered them quickly. "I can't see a damn thing, Kathie. The sun's too strong."

And then the engine was very loud and something came in, right in the path of that evening sun, like a great, black bird until it was almost above me. It dropped lower and lower, obviously deliberately; there was a roar as the engines were boosted. Even without the glasses I caught a glimpse of those Stars and Stripes of *Jenny Gone*. No damage, no black smoke. Johnny was safe.

Richie flew on towards the base, and my father put an arm around my shoulders. I said, "I've been really frightened all afternoon. Sick with fear. I was sure he must be dead. It wouldn't go away, that thought."

"It won't," he said gently. "Every time the same, Kathie."

I looked up at him. "And you don't think I can take it?"

"I think you're very young."

I managed a brave smile. "Who was it said in a sermon six months ago that in this war we've all got to learn to grow up quickly because there's a part for each and every one of us to play?"

He sighed and shook his head. "Ah, those sermons. Are they going to haunt me for the rest of my life?" He kissed me on the forehead. "I'll go and see if there's any tea going."

He went in, and I stood there watching the rim of the sun vanish behind the hill. The shadows lengthened; rooks called in the beech trees. So he was safe for now. *Until tomorrow.* The words rose unbidden. I pushed them away, turned and went inside.

I tried the piano for a while, but I sounded such an amateur after listening to Johnny that I abandoned it quickly and went into the kitchen. My mother was baking, flour up to her elbows, and my father was pouring tea into three cups. I could tell by the way he looked up that they had been talking about me.

"Just in time," he said.

My mother glanced over her shoulder, practical as always, not an ounce of sentimentality in her. "What about my roses?"

"Oh, my God," I said, which was hardly the kind of remark any well-bred rector's daughter should have been coming out with. "I forgot all about them."

I went into the garden and found the scissors and basket where I'd dropped them. The roses looked rather the worse for wear. I salvaged what I could and cut some more. *Where is he?* I was asking myself, and he hadn't even had time to take off his flying kit and have a drink.

I took the roses in and had my tea. Then I sat at the window with a book and waited. Half an hour passed, then an hour. It would be dark soon, and still no sign. I was hurt and angry. Surely he must know I would be waiting. As that thought took hold, I grew angrier still.

I'd been frightened all afternoon. I'd really thought he'd had it and it had cut me up more than a little, but I think there must have been more to my anger than that. The realization, perhaps, that I already cared for him too much for comfort.

My parents knew I was waiting, and I didn't want them to see how hurt and disappointed I was. I didn't want sympathy, so I let myself out of the house quietly, walked up to Hervey's and saddled Jersey Lil.

It was a stupid thing to do and dangerous in the fading light, but I was in the mood for a little danger, so I rode her fast across the top meadow and jumped three fences in an extremely foolhardy manner, coming to my senses soon enough and reining her in on the edge of the marsh. My neck was my own concern, but Jersey Lil was at least entitled to a choice.

There were tears in my eyes now, not entirely caused by the wind. I was tired and upset, yesterday's sleepless night catching up on me, and I always have had a tendency to build things up when overtired.

I took her back, cantering occasionally. Perhaps Johnny had arrived at the house while I had been away. That would be awful. I should be there. He'd been out over enemy territory and here was I complaining because he'd probably snatched a couple of hours' sleep. The ride had brought me to my senses.

When I turned in at the gate and went up the drive in the darkness, I could just make out the MG parked at the bottom of the steps. He *had* come, and I felt rotten for ever doubting that he would. I hurried into the hall, but there was no piano playing, not any kind of sound from the conservatory.

Someone was talking in the study. I hurried across the hall and opened the door quickly, but the smile on my face faded, for there was no sign of Johnny. Only my father and mother and Richie seated around the blazing log fire, a tea tray on the brass coffee table beside them.

My father said, "Ah, there you are."

Richie stood up and smiled. He looked very dashing in cream slacks and the brown battle-dress type of tunic American Air Corps officers often wore, but he seemed tired and there were dark smudges under his eyes.

"I wanted to make sure you knew we'd got back safely."

"I saw you fly over."

"A piece of cake, really," he said. "We were in and out again before they knew what hit them. A couple of ME-109s chased us on the way back, but Johnny shot one down so the other sheered off."

"Where is he?"

"Up at the base. Taking a shower, last I saw. I think he was going to turn in."

I didn't know what to say, and I was angry because I didn't understand. My mother poured tea for me. When she handed me the cup I avoided her eye deliberately.

There was an awkward silence and Richie, looking for

something to say, turned to my father. "You were a flier during the last war, sir?"

"That's right," my father said. "Very different in my day, of course. Seat-of-the-pants stuff. You took a ground-school course at Reading, aerial gunnery at Turnberry and finished up at the RFC school of aerial fighting at Ayre in Scotland, and all that only took a couple of months or so." He paused, sipping his tea meditatively, a faraway look in his eye. "There were a dozen of us in my class and six were American boys. All volunteers. September 1917. We flew Camels."

"I hear they were great planes," Richie said.

"But a devil to fly. They were so small that the big hundred-and-fifty-horse rotary engine would have you over before you knew what was happening. And you could never turn to the right because that was against the torque."

"It doesn't sound like my kind of action at all," Richie said with feeling.

"By the end of the course, six of the original twelve were dead, all from turning right instead of left, and that was before we got anywhere near the front. I was nineteen—just like Johnny."

Richie said, "Did you know that half the aircrew killed in the war so far haven't died in action, but as a result of accidents or crashes during training?"

"Something the powers that be aren't too keen for the public to know," my father commented.

There was silence. I could hear the bats calling shrilly to each other as they flitted between the trees outside. "Later on," my father said, "I flew SEs. Fastest things at the front. They used to say that if you survived the first ten days you stood a chance. I managed to hang on until February 1918; then I was shot down and broke both legs."

All this was new to me. He had never spoken of it before, and I sat staring at him, seeing a stranger; someone I had never known existed.

"It saved my life, of course," he went on. "If I'd had to fly out the rest of the war, I'd probably have died." He nodded as at some secret and private thought and started to fill his pipe. "You're on your third tour?"

"That's right, sir."

My father nodded. "Well, as I say, in my day, the longer you survived the better your chances. A question of experience, I suppose. That must still hold true."

"Only up to a point," Richie said. "You were on your own; responsible for your own destiny. These days it isn't a question of the man so much as the machine. You're up against more. That's the difference. And then there's your luck, and when that runs out . . . !" He got up. "I think I'll be getting back. It's been a hard day."

"Of course." My father shook hands. "Come again."

"I will, sir."

Richie turned to my mother, who handed him his cap. "Thanks for the tea, Mrs. Hamilton. See you again soon."

"I'll walk you to the car," I said.

When we went out through the front door it had started to rain again, but as he had the hood up it didn't really matter. We stood beside the MG for a moment. I said, "You share it, then?"

"If I have a date or something special he uses the bike. Turn and turn about. You know how it is."

A totally male world of special friendships and always to be denied to a woman. The notice on the gate said KEEP OUT.

"Why didn't he come, Richie?" I suddenly cracked completely and fell against him, putting my arms about his neck, holding on tight. "Why didn't he come?"

Reading the entry in my diary now, I wonder how I

could have been so naive. Poor Richie. Dear, dear Richie, and yet no Southern gentleman out of a Hollywood film could have behaved more gallantly.

"He gets these moods sometimes." He kissed me very chastely on the forehead. "You know something, Kate? This Big Brother act is very definitely not me. I'd better get the hell out of here."

He scrambled into the MG and started the engine. "Thanks, Richie. Thanks for coming." I leaned in under the hood and kissed him on the cheek impulsively.

He reached out and touched my face in the darkness. "He's a fool, that Johnny. Six different ways." I moved back, and as he drove away he called, "Don't worry, he'll be around."

But he didn't come. Not then and not during the rest of the week.

5

I WAITED ALL THAT LONG WEEK, hoping he would come, angry when he didn't and upset because I didn't know why. One problem was that I hadn't enough to do. I practiced the hymns for the Sunday service on the organ, exercised Jersey Lil, helped my mother when asked, but otherwise spent my time walking across the marshes alone, thinking a great deal. Not that my thoughts got me anywhere.

On Saturday afternoon after lunch I followed the main dike across the mud flats, the same route I had taken with Johnny on that last day, making for the shore. It was a gray sort of day, wind bringing a fine rain in off the sea, which suited my mood perfectly. I trudged along, hands pushed into the pockets of my old mac.

I was so bound up with my thoughts, so inside myself, that I didn't see the motorbike until I was right on top of it. I paused in surprise. It was Richie's machine, I was certain of that, the only difference being that it now had a sidecar attached with a canvas hood. For a wild moment I thought of Johnny and hurried forward, but it was Richie I found on the other side of the sand dunes.

He was wearing a heavy sweater and flying jacket and sat on a small collapsible canvas stool on top of the shingle bank in front of an easel. I don't think I've ever been so surprised in my life.

The pebbles rattled underfoot as I approached, and he glanced over his shoulder quickly, but kept on painting. "The secret life of Henri Richaud. Now you know all."

The painting was only half finished, but even so it took my breath away. He had the most remarkable feeling for form. Everything was entirely developed in paint without any preliminary sketch, one wash of color soaking into another. On the far side of the marsh an old mill had been standing for at least two hundred years. Now it was abandoned to wind and rain, and it stood up against the sky stark and gray. In Richie's painting it seemed even grayer, more alone. For some reason it hurt me to look at it. It made me think of Johnny.

"Quite a landmark to everyone at Upton Magna, that old mill," he said. "First thing I look for on the way in from the sea."

"I didn't know, Richie," I said. "About this, I mean," and for some reason I added, "I'm sorry."

He looked up at me, startled, then laughed. "You're a great girl, Kate, you know that? Don't let anyone change you." He laid down his tin of watercolors and took out his cigarettes. "You like it?"

"Oh, yes, it says everything I've ever felt about this place. Everything."

He grinned. "With me flattery gets you anywhere. When it's finished, you can have it."

"I couldn't."

"Don't be coy; it doesn't suit you," he said, rather sharply. He picked up his box of watercolors and started to paint again.

The rebuke lay between us like a barrier, and I sought

desperately for something to say. "Where did you learn to paint like that?"

"Back home in New Orleans. My grandfather gave me the foundations. Then I went on to Paris. I was there when the Germans moved in. As an American I was a neutral, of course, so they let me alone at first."

"What happened then?"

"Let's say I didn't like some of the things I saw. The final straw was my professor. He was a Jew, and they took him and his family away at an hour's notice. God knows what's happened to them. I made my way to Lisbon, caught a boat home, went straight up to Canada and joined the RCAF. I was flying my father's old Puss Moth at fifteen, took a pilot's license the moment I was old enough, so there was no problem. I was in England within three months undergoing operational training. The rest, as they say in the movies, you know."

I looked at the painting again. "What a waste," I said. "What a terrible waste."

He turned on me angrily. "Be your age, Kate. I fly because I chose to fly. There's a war on, in case you hadn't heard—mainly because a bunch of rather unpleasant gentlemen in fancy uniforms on the other side of the North Sea wanted to turn Britain into another slave market for the German Reich. That's what it's all about and don't you ever forget it. I was in Paris. I saw what happened. Maybe that's the difference between Johnny and me. I know that what we're doing has to be done. It's a fact of life."

"I'm sorry," I said.

He shook his head in exasperation. "What did you expect me to do? Stop painting because there's a war on; because I live in danger of being blown to hell and back tomorrow night? Well, that's what it is, Kate. Tomorrow, and this is today." He took a wallet from the inside pocket of his tunic and produced a folded piece of paper. "That's what I live by. I cut it out of a magazine a year ago."

It was a few lines from a poem of Robert Browning's. As I read them, I had to fight to hold the tears at the sheer, foolish gallantry of it.

> *I was ever a fighter so—one fight more,*
> *the best and the last!*
> *I would hate that Death bandaged my eyes*
> *and forbore*
> *And bade me creep past.*

I handed the scrap of paper back to him, turning my head away, and he stood up and put an arm around me, his voice full of concern. "Come on, kid. It's just a game. A black joke on somebody's part, but we all have to play along. No other choice." He tilted my chin. "A big smile for Uncle Richie and you might get something nice."

I put my hands on his shoulders. "You fool, Richie. You wonderful idiot. I could kiss you."

"Oh, no you don't," he said, standing back in mock alarm. "I think I can guarantee that would definitely be the very worst thing you could do." He unzipped his flying jacket and unfastened a small gold badge. "Ever seen one of these before?"

It was a gold caterpillar with ruby eyes. "Doesn't Johnny wear one on his tunic?"

"That's right. The Caterpillar Club, founded by a man called Irving who invented the world's first free-fall parachute. The first time you save your neck by jumping for it they send you one of these and enroll you in the club." He pinned it carefully into the lapel of my mac. "Something to remember me by."

I have it still—one of my very dearest possessions. Whenever I look at it, I stand again on the shore on that gray afternoon, the sound of the sea in my ears, rain on my face, and Richie . . .

I was full of emotion and walked a pace or two away from him. After a while, I turned. He was watching me gravely, waiting for the inevitable question. How cruel we are when we are young. How little I knew of the pain I caused Richie in those days.

"You said he'd come, but he hasn't."

"So what do you expect me to do?"

"What's he doing, Richie?" I demanded. "I've been waiting for a whole week. He's no right to behave like that. What's wrong with him? Doesn't he think about me at all? Doesn't he know the pain he's causing?"

"Johnny, Johnny, Johnny! That's all I ever seem to hear from you, and there are very definitely limits to friendship." He grabbed me by the arms painfully. "Why bother, Kate? Why do you women always have to try for the apple that's just out of reach?"

"Please, Richie."

He released me. His face had set in a hard, grim expression, his lips pressed firmly together as if to hold in his anger. "All right, sweetheart. You want to know about Johnny Stewart. I'll show you."

He dismantled his easel, put the painting and his gear into a large wooden box and set off along the shingle bank without another word. When we reached the motorbike he stowed everything away in the sidecar and turned to me.

"You can ride inside too. And keep your head down."

"But where are we going?" I demanded.

"Upton Magna. As your father would say on a Sunday: here beginneth the first lesson."

At the front gate they simply waved Richie through. I crouched down inside the sidecar, well hidden by the canvas hood, occasionally peeping out through the cracked Perspex side window. Finally, we braked to a halt; he switched off the engine, then pulled back the hood for me to get out. It was still raining. We were beside some hangars, but for the moment there seemed to be no one about.

"This is the quiet time," he said. "The ground crews won't be coming on for another hour yet to get ready for tonight."

"There's a raid on?" I said.

He nodded and walked towards the nearest hangar. A Lancaster was parked at one side, forlorn in the rain. She'd been badly shot up, the fuselage punctured in many places by flak and cannon shell, and one of the engines was a mass of twisted metal. The rear turret was shattered, the Perspex panels fragmented. The interior was completely wrecked, torn apart by machine-gun bullets. There were dark stains on the floor which told their own story. I felt sick and rather dizzy, and Richie put an arm around me.

"You wanted to know."

"I'm all right. Tell me what happened."

"They were attacking naval installations at Rotterdam. An hour across the North Sea, three or four minutes over target, an hour back. A milk run, only this time they were attacked by ME-109s on three occasions. The pilot took a bullet in the leg, but managed to bring her in. They had luck in large quantities."

"And the rear gunner?"

"They took what was left of him out of the turret when they got back."

"Oh, my God."

He exploded in a kind of anger—frustration, I suppose, or a rage against dying—and grabbed my arm. "All right, you asked for it."

He pushed me across the front of the hangar. Another Lanc stood on the far side, no sign of damage at all, not a mark on the fuselage until we went round to the tail. There was no rear turret—only a gaping hole, leaving belts of ammunition and hydraulic pipes hanging.

"Over the target you don't just have Jerry to worry about. You've also got bombs and incendiaries falling from the kites above you. This turret was sheered off by a falling bomb. When it went, the rear gunner went with it."

I was aware of a choking sensation and fought for air.

"What they call the hazards of the calling. Take Johnny, for instance. One ditching off Sheringham, which he survived thanks to the Cromer lifeboat, although it can't have been much fun being three hours in the waters of the North Sea in February. Three crash landings of one kind or another; and he's had to jump for it twice. Then there are his hands. Burned so badly, he almost lost the use of them. Shrapnel in the left arm. Not too important, that, except to someone who had hopes of making a living as a professional pianist."

I felt numb; totally shocked; quite unable to speak.

"Which explains why he's something of a walking miracle." And then he added with cold brutality, "Ten ops, Kate, that's the average life expectancy of a Tail-End Charlie, because even when the kites get back he's often chopped to pieces. Ten ops. Thirty in a tour, and for a rear gunner to complete one of those is like the stone rolling from the mouth of that cave on Easter morning. You know how many Johnny has done? Seventy. That makes him pretty well unique."

"Seventy?" I said dully.

"Which means twenty to go. What would you say his chances are—at a conservative estimate, of course?" He took me by the shoulders and shook me in anger. "And you dare to complain about his behavior. You should be bloody well ashamed of yourself."

I turned and was very sick indeed.

It took me quite a while to pull myself together, and Richie hovered, looking worried and contrite. "Look, I'm sorry," he said. "I didn't mean it to go like this. I'll take you home now."

"No," I said. "I'd like to have a look at Johnny's plane first."

"You've seen enough."

"Please, Richie. I want to see what it feels like to be in there."

He hesitated, then shrugged. "All right."

On the far side of the hangars half a dozen Lancs stood in a row, wing tips almost touching. Richie stopped beside the one at the end of the line. "There you are," he said. "B for Bertha, otherwise known as *Big Bertha*. Quite a famous old kite. Completed a hundred and one operations over enemy territory in her time. With different crews, of course." Underneath the cockpit window, rows and rows of bombs had been painted on the fuselage. "One bomb a mission."

A facsimile of the medal ribbon of a DSO and two DFMs had also been painted up there, and there were eight swastikas. "I see," I said. "Those medals have been earned by members of crews flying this plane."

"Exactly."

"Is Johnny's DFM up there?"

"No, he earned that in a Halifax. If there was any justice he should have had a bar to it by now. Two of those swastikas are his. One for each German fighter shot down."

"Is it true what they say about officer aircrew getting more medals than the NCOs?"

"I'm afraid so. You British are the biggest bunch of snobs I've ever come across. I got the bar to my DFC automatically for finishing my second tour. When you see a DFM you know it's been earned." He nodded up at the insignia. "The second one up there. That belongs to Bunny O'Hara, the present pilot. He's on his second tour. You met him at the dance."

"I don't remember."

"The pianist Johnny took over from. A mad Irishman from Cork who shouldn't even be in this war."

"People must have said much the same about you at one time."

"I suppose so." He shrugged. "Anyway, in you go."

He gave me a push up through the hatch into the interior of the Lancaster. "Go on," he said. "And watch your shins on the main spar."

Once inside I became aware of a rather strange smell and asked him what it was.

He grinned. "All Lancs smell like that. It's a mixture of paint, dope, metal, oil and the Elsan. Not so good if you have a delicate stomach."

I groped my way along the dark, narrow fuselage beneath the mid-upper gun turret sticking out of the roof. We came to the navigator's "office," as Richie termed it, the wireless operator's position, then up to the cabin.

To get into the bomb aimer's position in the nose I had to crawl down under the flight engineer's seat. I didn't like it much down there, although the view must have been quite spectacular in flight.

Richie said, "During takeoff and landing the bomb aimer's not supposed to stay in the nose for safety reasons, but most of them do. With parachute harness on it isn't easy to squeeze under the engineer's seat to get back into the front compartment."

I sat in the pilot's seat, dazzled by the multiplicity of

dials and controls. Richie tried to give me some idea of how it all worked, and then we moved back towards the rear, negotiating that main spar again. There was an Elsan closet, and finally the rear turret poking out between the rudders.

"They call this the loneliest place in the kite. Go in and sit down. You can shut the doors if you really want to know what it's like." There was a touch of mockery in his voice. I didn't reply, but got in and closed the doors firmly.

It was a peculiar sensation sitting in that confined space looking out at the ground below. Not that I could see much; the Perspex was scratched and the rain trickled down it. I put out my hands slowly to the handles of the machine guns. I was frightened that I might touch some mechanism and make them fire.

"Once inside there you're cut off from the others completely except by intercom." Richie's voice was muffled and indistinct.

I sat there for quite a while trying to imagine what it felt like to be up there, picturing a plane flying straight at you, wondering what it was like when you flew out at night and you were in the dark, alone, cut off from everyone else. It was unbearably quiet now. Yes, quite the loneliest place in the world.

I opened the doors. Richie was squatting there smoking a cigarette, something which I was to discover was very definitely forbidden. "It gets cold in there," he said, "especially with the center panel removed. As low as minus forty centigrade. Frostbite's another common occupational hazard. Johnny wears a kapok flying suit that's electrically heated, but often the heating system fails. That's when the hands go."

"But why take the center panel out?"

"Oh, it gets scratched or mists up. A lot of gunners

have died because they thought a Messerschmitt coming in fast from the rear was just a scratch on the Perspex."

"But to survive as long as Johnny has, he must be good," I said.

"With the guns?" He nodded. "None better. He was down for pilot training at first and soloed in Tiger Moths, but it wasn't his line. So they offered him navigator training or gunner. A nav's course takes around eighteen months to complete, a gunner's eight to ten weeks. Johnny, having some kind of death wish, made his choice."

"The DFM," I said. "How did he get that?"

"That's easy. I wrote the report. We were on our twenty-seventh operation. A night job, naturally. Ludwigshafen. Six and a half hours. It went badly from the start. Late over target owing to weather conditions, port outer damaged by flak. Somewhere over Holland we were attacked by an ME-109. Johnny was unable to fire because of a heating failure, but the intercom was still functioning so he was able to give me some sort of avoiding-action orders. The guy just kept coming in on our tail all the time, you see."

"And Johnny?"

"Made some kind of supreme effort in spite of frostbite in both hands. Got one of his guns to function and drove off the ME."

I reached again for the handles of the guns, trying to imagine what it was like. The lack of strength in those frozen hands.

"After that I thought we were home and dry, but halfway across the North Sea an FW-190 came right out of nowhere and knocked hell out of us."

"What happened?"

"A bloody shambles. The navigator was killed instantly; so was the bomb aimer. The wireless operator and mid-upper gunner wounded. The only turret which would function was the mid-upper, and that was on fire. My flaps were shot away, both rudders shattered and the tanks holed. That's where our German friend made his mistake. Thought he had us cold and came in too close, only Johnny had hauled himself into the mid-upper turret and was waiting for him."

"And shot him down?"

"That's right. Twenty minutes later we made it to the English coast by the skin of our teeth, and me being the great pilot I am, I put her down in a plowed field near Cromer."

"And Johnny?"

"He wasn't too healthy. Firing the guns in that burning turret hadn't done his hands much good, and he'd taken a bullet in the arm. The surgeons at the RAF burns unit did a great job on him, but it was never the same after that."

"What do you mean?"

"Before that we used to laugh about it. It was a game to be enjoyed, like being at college or something. In those days, everything was wizard or spot-on. We spoke about bagging a Hun and people pranging, as if it were all jolly good sport. But things changed. Too many people I used to know have died, Kate, so in the end . . ." He shrugged.

"What happened to Johnny after that?"

"He finished his tour, the other three ops, at Skellingthorpe with scratch crews. I met him again the day he went to Buckingham Palace for his DFM."

"You were there too?"

"That's right." Which was hardly surprising, for it seemed obvious that the part he himself had played in the affair must have earned him something.

"After that Johnny was made up to flight sergeant and posted to the Middle East. Flying Halifaxes from Egypt in raids against the Italian mainland. Not quite as rough as it is over here. The Italians don't really have their heart in it and their fighters aren't much good."

"And then he was sent home again?"

He nodded. "I was surprised when he turned up here. After completing a first tour, you can be called back for a second whether you like it or not, but third tours are always a matter of volunteering."

"Surely you have the answer to that if anyone does," I said. "Aren't you in exactly the same position yourself?"

"I don't know any better," he said with a quick grin, but those eyes weren't smiling.

"What is it, Richie?" I said. "Do you want to die—is that it? Are you looking for it?"

"Oh, no you don't," he said. "I never was one for that kind of philosophy. Ask your old man. Maybe he could use it as a theme for a sermon."

He turned and made his way back to the hatch and I followed. He helped me down to the ground. Two trucks arrived and unloaded ground crew in overalls. They scattered towards the various planes, and some of them looked curiously at Richie and me. They saluted briskly enough. But then, Richie was something special, as I was beginning to learn.

We stood beside *Big Bertha* and I looked up at those rows of bombs painted on the side. "What do I do, Richie?" I said without looking at him.

"That's up to you, kid."

"Yes, I see that now."

He put an arm about my shoulders. "Cheer up. It's a funny old world. As the song says, anything goes. Sometimes miracles can happen."

But I didn't believe him, not for a moment, and I turned my head into his shoulder as we walked back to the motorbike.

The solution when it came was so simple that I was astonished that I hadn't thought of it before. I couldn't wait to get home and didn't say a word to Richie, except to thank him when he dropped me at the front door.

When I went into the living room my parents were seated on either side of the fire having afternoon tea, wartime variety. Margarine, toast and homemade black currant jam. My mother looked up. "What have you been up to?"

There didn't seem to be any point in beating about the bush. I said, "I've been thinking, Mummy. You know how you keep telling me I don't have enough to do and so on?"

My father lowered his paper and peered over the top of his glasses. My mother looked wary. "Well?"

"I've got the perfect solution. You're always saying you need help with the WVS canteen at Upton Magna." I spread my arms. "Your problems are over."

My voice trailed away as I saw my father's face. There was a heavy silence. He took off his glasses. "It won't do any good, Kathie. If the lad doesn't want to see you, he doesn't want to see you and that's an end of it."

"It isn't as simple as that, Daddy—not anymore," I said. "I saw Richie this afternoon. He took me up to the base, showed me over Johnny's plane. And he told me things I just didn't know before. I understand it all so much more now. He thinks he's finished. He thinks there's nothing left for him. I want to show him there is."

He stared at me. It was my mother, of all people, who said gently, "She's right, you know, George. We are always short-handed on the night shift at the canteen."

My father said mildly, "She is also very young."

"But you said . . ." I started hotly, and he put up a hand.

"That young people have to learn to grow up quickly in wartime. All right, Kathie, spare me that."

"And she will always be with me," my mother pointed out. My father didn't answer, but busied himself filling his pipe. She added softly, "He's a nice boy, George."

He sighed. "I know when I'm beaten. There's no need for that kind of emotional blackmail." He turned to me. "All right, Kathie. Try it for a week. See how things go. But if it doesn't work out . . ."

I flung my arms about his neck and kissed him, then ran out to the conservatory and sat down at the piano. It was going to work because it *had* to. I was filled with excitement and started to play a Bach prelude, a favorite of Johnny's. I don't think I've ever played better.

It was cold that night, colder than it had been for some time, and in spite of my slacks and the thick sweater I wore under my mac, I felt it.

The whole thing got off to a bad start, for the simple reason that the planes left on schedule. During the early part of the night, there was only a demand for the tea and buns we provided at the WVS canteen when there were delays and the crews had to hang about dispersal, all kitted up and nowhere to go.

So I didn't see Johnny, not even in the distance. There were so many planes, after all—three squadrons—and the crews were taken out to the Lancasters by the truckload. The air was so filled with the noise of engines that you couldn't hear yourself speak. I stood beside the trailer and watched them take off very quickly, one behind the other.

Although it was ten o'clock it was quite light, thanks to double summer time, and I was able to follow them for quite a while before they dwindled into the dark haze on the horizon.

Old Mrs. Smith from the village stores was helping my

mother that night, and I heard her say, "Where are they going, then?"

Which was supposed to be confidential information, but everyone on the station knew. "Berlin," my mother said. "An eight-hour trip."

"Start seeing them coming back around five-thirty, then, depending on the weather."

We didn't have a single customer. I said to my mother, "Now what? Do we just wait?"

"Lord bless you, no," she said. "We'll have ground-crew lads swarming all over us in another five minutes. You'll have your hands full, believe me."

And she was right. Not that I minded. It gave me something to do, and everyone seemed so cheerful, even after midnight when it got colder and colder. But that was the way things went in wartime, people pulling together. I know it isn't a fashionable point of view now and I could be accused of romanticizing, but my diary tells me differently. We *did* pull together, because we had to. As Richie once said to me, everyone was going up the beach the same way.

Mrs. Smith slept from midnight until two-thirty in the narrow bunk at one end of the caravan trailer. When she got up, I took over the bunk and fell into instant sleep. The next thing I knew, I was being shaken gently by the arm.

"Wake up, Kathie. They're coming in," my mother was saying.

I was up in an instant, out of the door and standing outside. It was a quarter to six and very cold, but visibility was good. The first Lancaster was already landing, brakes squealing, and my mother called, "Come on, Kathie, work to be done."

There were sandwiches to lay out on the counter, milk to pour into dozens of cups, and already the first of the aircrews was trudging across the tarmac. From then on my hands were so full that I had little time to notice what was going on outside the immediate circle of the canteen. Lancasters were landing one after another, some with extensive damage. None of the aircrew who crowded about the counter seemed in the slightest bit worried, even when a plane with half its tail gone came in too fast and skidded off the runway, coming to a halt when its undercart collapsed.

There was a great ironic cheer. "Poor old Charlie, flat on his rear again," someone called, only he didn't say rear.

They all looked so tired, faces grimy, dark-circled from the goggles, and yet they were so incredibly cheerful. It was wrong somehow. It didn't make sense. I glanced up as another plane taxied up to dispersal and saw Richie walking towards me. He was in flying jacket and boots, cap on the back of his head as usual, and carried a parachute in one hand.

He waved, surprise on his face, and a WAAF corporal, whom I had noticed earlier getting out of the driver's seat of one of the trucks, ran towards him. He put an arm around her and kissed her briefly. As I found out later, she was a Belgian girl named Anne-Marie Perrier, one of the drivers from the transport pool who ferried the aircrews to debriefing and then to the mess for the ritual bacon and eggs.

And then I saw my father towards the back of the crowd, moving amongst them, handing out cigarettes, laughing and joking. He looked different, like someone else. It was as if I had never known before what he was truly like.

Things took a turn for the worst with astonishing suddenness. Another Lancaster came in too fast, overshot the runway at the far end and pancaked. There was some sort of explosion and nothing but action after that. Fire tenders, ambulances racing away, and I saw my father jump into the back of a passing jeep.

I stared out towards the blazing plane in horror and was aware of a hand on my sleeve, a voice speaking to me insistently. I came back to life with a start and looked down at a small, cheerful Australian air gunner. "Cup of tea, darlin'," he said. "I'm freezing."

I poured the tea, my mind numb. The men standing around were still laughing and talking amongst themselves, and beyond them the smoke rose. I didn't understand, and I should have done. Understanding came later.

I handed the Australian his tea and saw Johnny standing at the back of the crowd, staring at me in astonishment. He carried a parachute in one hand and had taken off his helmet, but there were great dark circles around the eyes from the goggles. I poured tea into a mug, opened the door and walked towards him.

I handed him the tea and said very deliberately, "Now what are we going to do?"

There was a slightly dazed look on his face. He turned as ammunition started to explode in the burning plane and watched, for a moment, the losing battle as the fire tenders fought to control the blaze. Ambulances roared past us making for the base hospital, probably with my father inside one of them.

"In the midst of life, eh?" Johnny said.

"A waste of breath," I told him. "We live, we die, just like the seasons. Spring, summer, autumn declining into winter. Not separate, but part of the whole." I saw that Richie had moved close and was listening. Johnny was staring at me impassively, retreating behind that bleak, cold emptiness again. I got angry then. "All right. You should have died a year ago or last week. It's a miracle you're here at all. So what are you doing? Are you thanking God for every extra day and getting on with living?

You should be ashamed, Johnny Stewart. You may be dead tomorrow, but you're alive today."

Richie clapped his hands. "Bravo!" he said. "Give the young lady a prize."

But Johnny just stood there staring at me, eyes dark, and I turned and marched back to the canteen.

I slept late and was awakened by music just after eleven. I put on my dressing gown and went down, pausing outside the conservatory door to listen. It was his own music he was playing, and my heart lifted.

When I went into the kitchen my mother handed me a tray without a word, but she smiled in a way I'd never seen before. When I went into the conservatory, I was almost floating.

He was seated at the Bechstein in his shirt sleeves, a pencil between his teeth as he played. He paused to make some correction to the manuscript in front of him, but made no sign of being aware of my presence. I poured a cup of tea and put it on top of the piano where he could reach it, then picked up his tunic and hung it over the back of a chair.

"Thanks," he said, glancing at me briefly.

No mention of last night. Not a word.

"Are you on tonight?"

"No, the met forecast for central Europe is the worst this month."

"Perhaps you'd like to go for a walk later on."

At first I thought he hadn't heard me, as he continued to play, and then he said, "Yes, I'd like that."

He leaned over the manuscript, frowning, and made a correction. I went out quietly, closing the door gently behind me.

6

Nimbus is the Latin word for rainstorm, and *cumulus* means heap and is used by weathermen to describe those puffy white clouds that shape up like mountains in the sky on a summer's day. *Cirrus* stands for curl or ring-let—feathery wisps of white ice crystals high in the sky, moving rapidly on winds, five or ten miles up. Often storm warnings. A danger sign for fliers everywhere, but not as much as cumulonimbus clouds—black, swollen, edged with pink and always indicating a violent thunderstorm.

In the weeks that followed I became familiar with all this—the jargon of the weathermen that could mean life or death to the Lancaster crews. Wind force five on the Beaufort scale meant fresh breeze; seven, moderate gale. *Whole trees in motion, sea heaping up, foam begins to streak.*

These were things Johnny and Richie knew by heart, the language of their daily lives. I learned them too, so that before very long I could tell by looking out at the weather if a bombing run was on or off that night.

I was at the base three or four nights a week now with

my mother, working at the canteen as the bombing offen-
sive against the Ruhr targets intensified, and it all quickly
became a part of my life. Planes going out, coming in
again in the dawn light. The aircrews, all of them so
young when I look back, the faces one got to know so
well, there one night and missing next morning. But crying was out, for there were just not enough tears to go
round.

Suddenly I knew the difference between the port outer
engine and the starboard. I knew that those engines were
Rolls-Royce Merlins, that the Lancaster had a range of
two thousand seven hundred miles and a bomb load of
four thousand pounds. And most important, the machine
guns that Johnny used were .303 Brownings.

Richie even made me learn some of the pilot's drills by
heart, and to this day I can recite them like a strange kind
of poetry.

Ready to start starboard inner.
Ground/Flight Switch—*On ground.*
Throttles—*Set.*
Pitch—*Fully fine.*
Slow Running—*Idle Cut off.*
Super-charger—*M gear—lights out.*
Air Intake—*Cold.*
Rad. Shutters—*Auto.*
No. 2 Tank—*Selected—booster pump on.*
Master Fuel Cocks—*On.*
Ignition—*On.*
Contact!

Johnny's logbook became my bible, for as well as details of all his training, the courses he had taken, every
hour he flew was entered there with all the targets in-
dicated. Blue for a daylight raid, red for night. The names

of those targets became as familiar to me as those of the Norfolk villages around my home. Hamburg, Bremen, Dortmund, Kiel. A round trip to Essen took five hours; Dortmund—five and a half; Ludwigshafen—six and a half; Berlin—eight. Dresden was the longest, at ten hours. I thought *that* night would never end.

The more I saw of the crews, the less I worried, for I became infected with their special brand of fatalism. I saw that some people only lasted a few weeks while others seemed to go on for ages. By now, of course, I was totally accepted as a fixture at the WVS canteen, and I got to know Johnny's crew particularly well.

There was Flight Sergeant Bunny O'Hara, the Irishman, always playing hell about the *bloody* English, as he called us, for what they had done to Ireland. I could never quite make this fit with the fact that he had volunteered for the Royal Air Force. No one ever seemed to ask him why. They just accepted his ranting, joked about it and ignored it. That was one thing about aircrew; they tolerated each other's peculiarities; and Bunny did have a DFM, which helped.

Richie used to say that most of them were half mad anyway by the time they had completed a tour and told me a nasty story about a Polish rear gunner on his third tour who used to regularly knock his head against the iron pipe on the hut stove. It upset me considerably for a day or two.

The rest of the crew of *Big Bertha* were just as individual as Bunny. There was Dad Walker, the flight sergeant navigator, so-called because he was thirty and easily the oldest man in the crew. He had designed sets for a theatrical company before joining the RAF. He'd done a wonderful painting of a Lancaster on the wall of the NCOs' mess.

The wireless operator was a West Indian from Bar-

bados, Henry Maclaine, and his pal was a little Scot called
Billy Forbes, the mid-upper gunner. George Middleton,
the bomb aimer, never told anyone his background,
which was hardly surprising. Some years later I discovered that he had been an ordained minister of the Meth-
odist Church. Last of all was Ted Ormeroyd, the flight
engineer, a Lancashire lad from Preston who could play a
ukulele banjo like George Formby and knew most of
his songs, too, although when he tried to sing "It's in the
Air" in the NCOs' mess they debagged him.

Except for Bunny and Dad and Johnny they were all
sergeants and all on their first tour, although as Johnny
had had two in hand when he joined them, he was due to
finish before they did. They were a rough lot, always joking, beer and girls the main topics of conversation. But
they all treated Johnny with respect, even Bunny, for as
Richie had told me, he was something of a legend.

And they were superstitious, like most aircrew. Just before leaving on a mission they used to touch Johnny's
sleeve for luck, a ritual started by Ormeroyd. And he
never seemed to mind, which surprised me.

But he was happy then—happier than I had ever known
him. He came regularly to the house to work at his music,
often accompanied by Richie, so that both of them became rather like fixtures at the rectory. We even reached
the stage where my father actually stopped calling Richie
Captain Richaud, so I knew finally that miracles can happen.

I spent all my spare time with Johnny. We borrowed a
horse for him from another farm nearby and went riding
on the marsh. He was good, but Jersey Lil was the better
mount so I usually won our races.

Often, on evenings when Johnny wasn't on, we'd drive
into Fakenham to visit the cinema in the marketplace.
Richie used to come too, although he never brought his

WAAF corporal, Anne-Marie, with him, which puzzled me. I suspect now, at a distance in years, that the kind of relationship he enjoyed with her was something he wanted to keep separate, perhaps from me.

On the twenty-seventh of July we celebrated Johnny's birthday by going to see a film called *Dangerous Moonlight* about a Polish concert pianist, now a fighter pilot in the RAF, torn between his desire to shoot down Germans in revenge for what they had done to Warsaw and his need to compose his concerto. Richie and Johnny behaved disgracefully, making loud and ribald comments about the fake flying sequences and the noble Anton Walbrook. At one point the manager appeared and threatened to have us thrown out, although his attitude changed rather when the usherette flashed her torch and he saw the flying uniforms.

But they liked the music. As we walked out into the square, Richie said, "You and Anton do have one thing in common, Johnny. He had his *Warsaw Concerto*; you've got your *Norfolk Rhapsody*."

And there was its title, just like that. Richie became more involved in the *Rhapsody*, as it became from that moment, than I'd realized was possible. One afternoon I walked into the conservatory after shopping in Fakenham with my mother to find them both there. Johnny was playing away and Richie, a cigarette in his mouth and a look of intense concentration on his face, was sitting on the other side of the piano, copying it all neatly out in manuscript.

I hadn't realized that he'd had a certain amount of musical training. I suppose that somehow, I hadn't thought of a drummer as being a real musician, which shows just how much I had to learn.

But it was a bad time in many ways. Bomber Command was suffering terrible losses over the Ruhr, the worst of the war. Too many planes were being lost; too many good men were dying.

At first, the way the aircrews treated the deaths had seemed callous, but I realized soon enough that this wasn't so. They simply couldn't afford to wear their hearts on their sleeves. When someone said, "Oh, he got the chop" or "They bought it over Hamburg" in a casual, bright voice, he wasn't being cruel. It was the only way to get through a time of such heavy losses; otherwise the morale of the whole base would have simply gone to pieces.

It couldn't last, of course—my happiness and Johnny's. In the second week of August, when he still had seventeen ops to go, came the biggest raid on Hamburg yet, and it continued the following night. Bomber Command lost a hundred and three Lancasters on those two nights alone.

I remember the second night well—one of the most terrible of my whole life. We were waiting at Upton Magna for the planes to come in, and because of the previous night's losses the tension was tremendous. It was dawn when they started to arrive, a pale light on the horizon, swooping in one after another. Many of them had been badly knocked about.

There were three crash landings. Two made it successfully, but the third lost its undercarriage halfway down the runway and slued to one side, smashing into two planes which had just landed. Luckily, their crews had already got out, but there was a bad fire, smoke rising in a great black cloud. A stiff breeze carried it across the base, so that it hung over everything like a dark pall.

It was the first time I got the impression of real chaos. Fire tenders and ambulances and all sorts of different trucks appeared haphazardly from the smoke. The air-

crews at the canteen weren't smiling this morning. Things
had been too bad.

I was working my way through them carrying a tray
loaded with mugs of tea and paused on the edge of the
crowd to look up above the smoke to where the last three
or four Lancasters to come in were making their circuit.
Then I saw another plane, one that was entirely unfamil-
iar to me. Two-engined, painted black, strange aerials
sticking out from the nose.

It dived in fast behind the last Lancaster in line, coming up beneath it, and there was a rattle of cannon fire. As
it swung away, the Lancaster lurched and dived straight
into the ground on the far side of the airfield.

There was a stunned silence from the men around me,
and then a voice boomed over the Tannoy from the
tower, "Take cover! Take cover!"

Another black plane exactly like the first came in
through the smoke no more than a hundred feet above
the ground, so low that I could see the German crosses on
the wings and fuselage, the swastika on the tail plane. It
released two bombs and continued along the runway,
cannon shell and machine-gun bullets ripping up the
ground, hammering into the parked Lancasters.

There was complete panic, an ugly thing to see—people
running everywhere. I didn't know where my mother
was. I dropped my tray and stood there frozen to the
spot, and then there was a hand on my arm and someone
screamed, "Get down! Get down, you fool!"

I was dragged backwards with such force that I fell
over and found myself lying beside Anne-Marie Perrier.
Another of the black planes swept in, guns firing
furiously, and I tried to get to my feet to run for the shel-
ter of a truck.

She pulled me back down. "No, we're safer in the
open."

There was more machine-gun fire; then the engines roared away, receded into the distance. As I heard later, JU-88 night fighters, on a carefully planned hit-and-run attack. They'd taken off from bases in Holland and joined on at the end of the returning bomber stream, holding back their attack until the Lancasters were landing at their home bases and were sitting ducks. Eleven bomber stations in Norfolk and Lincolnshire were hit in the same way on that dreadful morning.

There was silence now—only the crackling of flames—and then the second of the fire tenders and ambulances going into action again. People lay on the ground all around me, most of them dazed, shocked by the unexpectedness of it all. The entire attack couldn't have taken more than three or four minutes.

There was smoke everywhere, and I could hear a scream. A gust of wind tore a gap in the dark curtain, revealing a burning truck. There was a man in the cab. I could see his face at the window as he vainly tried to get the door open.

Anne-Marie was on her feet and running. I saw her reach the truck, jump on to the running board and wrench at the handle of the door with all her strength. In the same moment I heard the engines roaring again as another JU-88 came in low. Surely someone would help her —but as machine-gun bullets ripped up the tarmac again everyone stayed down.

The truck was burning fiercely now. I don't think I've ever been so frightened in my life—and yet suddenly I found myself up and running towards her. I was aware of the German plane flashing past again on the far side of the truck, so close that I could see two men in the cockpit, and then a hand in the back sent me sprawling on my face.

"For Christ's sake, get back!"

It was Johnny, and ahead of him Richie was running. Anne-Marie had the door open and fell back, pulling the driver out with her. Richie shoved her out of the way. As Johnny arrived, they picked the man up between them, turned and ran.

Anne-Marie was running too and grabbed my arm, urging me on. The roar of the engine of the last JU-88 dwindled away. A moment later, the truck's petrol tank exploded.

They put the truck driver on the bunk in the WVS canteen and Richie darted away in search of an ambulance. I gazed about me wildly. There was no sign of my mother, and I pushed through the crowd looking for her.

There was nothing—nothing but smoke and the crackle of unseen flames. The wreckage of planes hit on the ground, one hangar in ruins, dust-shrouded rubble. Over everything, a rising column of smoke.

The acrid smell of burning sickened me, and all around men were emerging, dazed and shocked, gazing at the chaos and ruins as if unable to take it in. The fire tenders were back at work now, the ambulances on the move.

I returned to the canteen and found my mother immediately. Her face was blackened, and she had a cut on her forehead. She flung her arms around me and hugged me tight.

"What about Daddy?" I said.

"He's all right. Very worried about you, but he's gone up to the hospital. He had to, dear."

The side door of the canteen opened and Johnny stepped out. He was still in flying gear, and his face was black from the smoke, eyes wild. He grabbed me by the arms. "You little fool."

I pulled away from him, still dazed. I felt tired. Too

tired to argue. I just wanted to lie down. I reached for the handle of the canteen door.

Johnny pulled me back. "Don't go in there."

"Why not?" I said.

"The truck driver's dead."

It was astonishing how quickly Upton Magna got back on its feet again. New Lancasters were delivered within a matter of days to replace those damaged beyond repair; bulldozers and enormous concrete-laying machines appeared as if by magic to repair the damaged runways.

I had one bad moment the following morning when my father came home from the base hospital, where he had stayed all night to help comfort the wounded and dying. He was very tired, his face drawn and haggard. I think it was the first time I had seen him look his age.

My mother and I were in the kitchen. He kissed her briefly, but I noticed that they held hands very tightly for a long moment. Then he turned to me and held out his arms.

After a while, he said, "No more, my dear."

I looked up at him. "You mean you don't want me to go on helping at the canteen?"

"That's right."

"And Mummy? Presumably you won't want her going up anymore, either?"

He sighed heavily. "Only two weeks to your seventeenth birthday, Kathie. I'd like to feel you might live to see it."

I said, "It's a matter of age, is it? All right if Mummy gets the chop, but not me."

His eyes widened, perhaps at my use of RAF slang. It was my mother who said quietly, "She has a point, George. We're in this together, all of us."

"I remember another of your sermons," I said. "The

one when you told us that this war was different. This time the civilians had to be prepared to fight too."

Something went out of him, or perhaps he was simply very tired. "You know, Kathie, I really am getting close to the point of swearing off sermons for the rest of my life." He kissed me on the forehead. "And now, I must go to bed before I fall down."

He walked to the door and my mother went with him. As he opened it, he paused and turned back to me. "By the way, that young Belgian, the WAAF corporal, Anne-Marie Perrier. She's received an immediate award of the Military Medal."

The door closed behind them and for a moment the air in the kitchen seemed tainted by the smell of burning. I went out to the conservatory terrace and breathed in the freshness of the garden for a while, but it was a long time before that smell no longer returned to haunt me.

On the following Sunday my father persuaded Johnny to play the hymns for morning service at St. Peter's. He came to the house early and did an hour on the *Rhapsody*. I sat in the conservatory listening. It was good, very good indeed, there was no doubt about that; one could only imagine what one of the great concert pianists would do with it; but it still wasn't right. I knew it and so did Johnny. Something essential was missing, something very simple. A single piece of the jigsaw that would suddenly make sense of the whole picture. But at least he wasn't depressed about it and that was the main thing.

He'd even persuaded Richie to come to church. I was astonished when he appeared on the doorstep in his best uniform, looking terribly handsome and dashing. At the church he stubbornly insisted on sitting in the rear pew on his own. I stood beside the organ, turning the pages for Johnny, lending only half an ear to my father's sermon.

At one point I glanced over the heads of the congregation to Richie sitting there at the back. To my surprise there was a look of intense involvement on his face as he listened to what my father had to say. But then he noticed me watching and spoilt it all by winking deliberately.

Johnny played a Bach prelude as the congregation moved out, and Richie waited for us. It had been gray and overcast earlier, but now the sun had come out and the church was flooded with light. It made everything look different, including Johnny.

He turned to smile at me, and I became aware of the dark circles under the eyes, the tiredness. When he stood up, his shoulders sagged. I was suddenly bitterly angry with myself. Stettin the night before, which meant he'd been cooped up in that rear turret for just over eight hours, arriving back at base by six-thirty. And he'd been at the rectory by nine to play for me before coming here.

I took his arm. "You look tired, Johnny. What you need is some sleep. You can use my room. You know we have a late lunch on Sundays."

"Nonsense," he said. "I'm fine."

But he wasn't. Not then or in the days that followed. The inescapable fact seemed to be that he was spending too much time on his music and with me and simply not sleeping enough.

When I discussed it with Richie, he didn't try to make it look any better than it was. "You're right," he said. "Out four nights a week on average—five last week, if you remember. The rest of the time he spends working on that damned *Rhapsody* or with you. It doesn't pay to get too tired in our line of work, Kate. It affects the reflexes. When a Tail-End Charlie gets so tired he thinks a

Messerschmitt coming up astern is a fly on the Perspex, he's had it. It only takes one mistake."

"But what can I do?" I asked him.

Richie shrugged. "Your problem, kid. You had one once before and came up with the right answer. You'll think of something."

But before I could, events took care of the situation for me.

My seventeenth birthday was on the twentieth of August. *Big Bertha* died two nights later.

It should have been easy. What Johnny called a milk run. Oil installations outside Amsterdam. An hour across the North Sea, a few minutes over the target and home again. The German night fighter which attacked them a few miles west of Den Helder had other ideas. The RAF were losing a lot of bombers at that time whose crews never even knew what hit them. Apparently the JU-88s had been fitted with some kind of special machine gun which fired upwards at an angle, which meant they could attack from below.

The first thing they knew about the attack was when cannon shell ripped open the floor. What happened then is something I have only read about, for Johnny would never discuss it. My father managed to borrow a copy of Bunny O'Hara's account of the incident and brought it home to show me.

22/8/43. Self and crew. Op No. 16 Amsterdam. 2h 10m (night). Attacked from below by JU-88-G 15 miles west Den Helder. Nav. and W/Op killed instantly. N/F attacked again from starboard killing M/Upper gunner and badly wounding F/E. Compass U/S, elevator trim tabs U/S and kite kept wallowing. Windscreen shattered and I was hit in the left shoulder. N/F made third pass from starboard. By this time B/G had come forward to take up position in M/U turret and succeeded in shooting N/F down. Oxygen supply U/S and cold air coming in through shattered cockpit freezing. R/G managed radio contact with base. Luckily I had memorized the course and returned by Pole Star and moon. Lost height very rapidly and B/A and R/G between them helped me fly the kite. S/Outer engine U/S, P/Outer caught fire 15 miles east of Docking on Norfolk coast at 2000 feet. Contact made with Air Sea Rescue Hudson 5m later. Controls U/S. Impossible to ditch. B/A jumped. F/Es parachute U/S. Ordered R/G to jump. He refused. Lashed F/E to him with length of rope and he exited through floor hatch holding F/E in his arms. I followed immediately. Two ASR launches alerted earlier were already in the vicinity and I was picked out of the sea at 05.52 hrs. R/G and F/E well and in good condition except for F/Es wound.

So there it was in the sparse, technical language of an official report that somehow highlighted the drama even more. What it came down to in plain terms was that Johnny had jumped holding Ted Ormeroyd in his arms. Not the first time it had happened successfully, and falling into the sea must have helped.

Bunny was immediately awarded a bar to his DFM. And Johnny? Earlier that year a new medal had been introduced into the Royal Air Force for airmen of non-commissioned rank to take care of those situations where the powers-that-be couldn't make their minds up whether or not to award the Victoria Cross. It was called the Conspicuous Gallantry Medal, and I suppose Johnny's was amongst the first to be awarded.

The really important thing that came out of it all was the fourteen days' survivor's leave he received, although as Richie put it, it seemed a damned hard way of earning a couple of weeks off.

7

JOHNNY'S RIBBON for his CGM looked very well indeed. It was light blue with dark blue edges and it had to be sewn on all his tunics before the DFM ribbon, over which it took precedence. My needlework has never been up to much and my mother took care of that department. As I watched her do it, seated at the kitchen table, her glasses on the end of her nose, it was obvious that her pride was personal.

The change in Johnny on the first day of his leave was remarkable. There was a complete absence of strain, as if the strings had been cut. He was relaxed and happy, if tired. He didn't have any plans for going away, and it was my father who insisted he spend the whole of his leave at the rectory. We made up the spare room for him. The first day he slept for sixteen hours. The day after, for twelve. It was a week before he found eight hours enough.

We rode together, fished, even swam in the creek when the tide was up, in spite of all that black mud. Johnny said he liked to feel it squelch between his toes. We walked frequently across the marshes; and there was the *Rhapsody*, of course. He spent a great deal of time working on it and the house was full of music.

Towards the end of the week he suggested we go up to the hospital to see Ted Ormeroyd and Bunny. It wasn't a very pleasant experience and what I saw there shook me badly. I knew there would be wounds, but simply hadn't realized the nature of so many of them.

When we went into the foyer, there was a man in a dressing gown, his left arm in a sling, sorting through the magazines on the rack. When he looked up, I saw him clearly in the mirror on the wall and fought to control the panic that rose inside me at the horror of it.

He had a kind of plastic face, skin stretched very tight, shining in the light. The mouth was just a crease, the nose a misshapen blob of flesh. Everything seemed without foundation, twisted and out of shape.

He swung round and shook his magazine at Johnny, who clapped him on the shoulder. "Now then, gorgeous, how goes it?"

The little slit mouth opened; an unintelligible grunting emerged. "My girl friend, Kate Hamilton." Johnny waved at me. "You know her old man. The padre."

The face turned towards me. The mouth twisted in a ghastly smile, but the eyes were full of pain as if looking for the repugnance, the horror. Suddenly, all fear left me and I was filled with a burning sense of shame.

"Hello." I took the claw that was extended to me. "We've come to see Bunny O'Hara and Ted Ormeroyd."

"Number Three," he said quite distinctly, but very slowly, enunciating each word with great care, and nodded along the corridor.

"Keep smiling." Johnny patted him on the face and moved off along the corridor. We turned a corner. I paused, leaning against the wall to get control of myself again. He said, "You all right?"

"I think that's the cruelest thing I've ever heard you say," I told him. "To call that wretched man gorgeous."

He looked genuinely bewildered. "But that's his name. Gorgeous George Jackson." He frowned. "Or would you rather we made it Ugly George?"

I slumped down on to a bench against the wall. "It's no good, Johnny. I thought I was beginning to understand. Your attitude, how you all think . . ."

He sat down beside me. "George is from our other wing at Padbourne. That's why you've never seen him before. Got shrapnel in his arm on the last Hamburg run. He was a Spitfire pilot during the Battle of Britain. The trouble with those babies is when you get fire in the cockpit, especially if you have difficulty getting the canopy open. Then you fry, like George. He was lucky. He came down in the sea, which helped. I met him first at the burns unit at East Grinstead. They've done miracles for people like him." He spread out his hands. "When you come to think of it, not too bad a job in my case, either."

I seized his right hand and kissed it. "I should be ashamed."

"That's right," he said callously. "Now let's go and see Bunny and Ted."

As we went into Number Three Ward there were further shocks. Someone with bandaged eyes, tapping his way out of the door with a stick, lurched into Johnny, apologizing heavily. It was only when he heard the voice that Johnny recognized who he was. A further painfully bright conversation took place.

Inside, a boy lay sleeping in the first bed, the face on the pillow very pale. Under the blankets there was just a box frame where the legs had been. The chap in the next bed, who also greeted Johnny cheerfully, had lost his left arm above the elbow.

Johnny didn't bother to introduce me, and I stood at the end of the bed, an inane smile on my face. As we walked away, he said, "Know what he was doing in civvy street? Training to be a golf professional. Now, that's ironic if you like."

I felt even sicker, but more than that, my fear was returning. Johnny, as if sensing the situation, took my arm and said softly, "Try and hang on, there's a good girl. It won't take long."

There was no sign of Bunny, but Ted was lying in the end bed. His eyes were closed and he looked very weak indeed. Johnny glanced at me and shook his head, and we started to tiptoe away. Ted's eyes flickered open. There was a ghost of a smile on his face.

"Hello, there," he said.

Johnny's reply was unprintable. What is known in some quarters as good old-fashioned Anglo-Saxon. I'd never heard him use such language. He added, "Kate's here."

Ted reached for my hand, and I leaned down and kissed him. "You've got a right one here, Kate," he whispered. "Hang on to him, love, if you have any sense. Don't let go."

He closed his eyes, obviously laboring under intense strain. Johnny murmured, "You rest now, Ted. We'll come back and see you again."

Ted's eyelids twitched. "Don't worry about me, Johnny. I'm fine. They've had it. They can't touch me now. Not anymore."

As we moved away, a young flight lieutenant surgeon entered, a white coat open over his uniform. Johnny said, "Excuse me, sir, might I ask you how Ted Ormeroyd is doing?"

The doctor's eyes took in the medal ribbons. "Oh, yes," he said. "You're Stewart, the chap who jumped with him. He's got shrapnel in the left lung, but he's going to be fine. It will take time, of course, but one thing's certain. He'll never fly again. Won't be able to stand the altitude."

"You mean he's out of it?" Johnny asked.

"Oh, yes, nothing more certain." The doctor grinned. "If you're looking for that pilot of yours, O'Hara, I just saw him in the rest room. We're discharging him in the morning."

We went out of the ward. To my amazement, Johnny leaned against the wall for a moment, laughing. "What's so funny?" I demanded.

"Good old Ted," he said. "Don't you see, Kate? He's out of it. I mean to say, he's going to live, and I really mean live. Don't you think that's absolutely bloody marvelous?"

Suddenly, with all my heart, I wished it were Johnny lying in there—a little battered perhaps, even maimed, but at least certain of life.

We found Bunny sitting at a coffee table in the corner of the rest room playing solitaire, his left arm in a sling. He was delighted to see us, grabbed Johnny's hand with great enthusiasm and insisted on kissing my cheek.

"I'm fine," he assured us. "Just a flesh wound, like Errol Flynn in all those Hollywood movies."

"I hear they're discharging you tomorrow," Johnny said, giving him a cigarette.

"That's right. Fourteen days' sick leave and then back to the bloody mincing machine." He clapped Johnny on the shoulder. "You won't let them allocate you to another crew before I get back, Johnny?" In spite of that Irish grin, his voice was anxious. "I'm counting on you. I mean, we're going to see this thing through together, aren't we?"

"You're damned right we are." Johnny punched him in his good shoulder. "What are you going to do with your leave? Go home?"

Bunny nodded. "It's all laid on. They've arranged a lift

for me on a transport plane to Limavady, in the north of Ireland. I'll go south by train from there."

"Will you be coming back on the mail boat?"

"Am I, hell," Bunny said. "It would be just my luck to choose one a U-boat commander had got his eye on. No, I'll come back the same way. Have you seen Ted?"

"Just now."

"You know, then?" Bunny grinned. "Lucky old devil." He shuffled the cards awkwardly because of his sling. He wasn't smiling now. "There's just one thing, Johnny. Before I go tomorrow I have to see Dad's widow. I was hoping you might go with me." He hesitated. "Maybe you could come too, Kate?"

"Yes, of course," I replied automatically. I hadn't even known that Dad was married.

"The woman's touch. Might help things along a bit." He smiled, looking as if a load had been taken off his mind.

"We'll pick you up here in the morning, then," Johnny told him. "Ten o'clock all right?"

"Fine." The cramped fingers of his left arm proved incapable of coping with the pack of cards and they scattered across the table. He looked up and grinned. "Would you look at that? Do you suppose there's a chance it could get worse?"

Some aircrew, especially those whose wives had children so young that they were unable to work or join up, would try to arrange lodgings for them close to each airfield they were posted to. Dad Walker had managed to rent a cottage only a fortnight earlier in a village called Borfield, five miles from Upton Magna towards Holt. There hadn't even been time for him to introduce his wife to the crew.

It was a warm, rather pleasant day, but I was hardly looking forward to the experience for obvious reasons. To make matters worse, when we drew up outside the cottage gate there was a little girl playing in the garden on an improvised seesaw. She couldn't have been more than four or five.

"This is it," Bunny said, but made no move.

Johnny climbed over the car door and I went after him. Bunny followed reluctantly and opened the garden gate. The little girl sat motionless, watching us. As we went up the path I hung on to Johnny's arm. The front door stood open, and Bunny knocked.

"Hello the house. Anyone at home?"

"Yes?" A tall, red-haired woman of perhaps twenty-eight or -nine appeared at the top of the stairs and started down. "Can I help you?"

"Mrs. Walker?" Bunny took off his cap. "I'm Bunny O'Hara. I was Dad's skipper. And this is Johnny Stewart."

"I was in the crew too, Mrs. Walker. Rear gunner," Johnny said. "I'm sorry we didn't get a chance to meet before."

"No, I've been so busy settling in."

She stood there as if uncertain what to say, dreadfully calm. The little girl squeezed past us and ran to her. Bunny and Johnny were obviously at a loss. I took a deep breath and put out my hand. "I'm Kate Hamilton, Mrs. Walker. I was a friend of Dad's too. I work at the WVS canteen at the airfield. We wondered if there is anything we can do."

"Not really," she said in that toneless voice. "We're leaving on the afternoon train." She gazed about her. "I want to get away from this place as soon as possible."

There was a heavy silence. Johnny said awkwardly, "Look, Mrs. Walker, if there's anything—anything at all . . . Maybe we could help you pack . . ."

She cut in on him sharply, her eyes blazing. "There's only one thing you can do for me, Sergeant, which is to go away as quickly as possible. Can't you see your presence can do only one thing? Remind me that you are alive and he is dead?"

Johnny took an involuntary step back. "I'm sorry. . . ."

"You fool," she said. "Don't you see? There are times when kindness hurts far more than cruelty. It's the last thing I need now."

And I understood—perfectly. I pulled Johnny and Bunny away, shoved them out of the door and turned to her. "Goodbye, Mrs. Walker, and good luck."

Her face was calm again. She stroked her little girl's hair. She said tonelessly, "That young man—the gunner? You're in love with him?"

"Yes," I said calmly.

"Then you're the one who is going to need the luck."

It was perhaps the cruelest thing she could have said to me—rising up from the pain, the rage in her own broken heart, and instantly regretted. She started to shake.

I put my arms about her and kissed her gently on the cheek. "It's all right," I said. "I understand. Truly I do."

She broke down then, great sobs tearing at her. I went out quickly, closed the front door and returned to the MG. Johnny was already behind the wheel and Bunny crouched in the rear space. "God," he said, "but I need a drink after that."

I climbed in and Johnny put a hand on mine for a moment. "All right?"

"Fine," I said. "It's that poor woman I'm sorry for."

As he drove away, her words circled endlessly in my brain and refused to go away.

When we got back to the village, we went into the George. Bunny and Johnny went into the bar and I slipped into the parlor. It was always quiet at that time of day, and just now I felt like a little peace. As I sat down, I noticed someone standing in the shadows at the end of the tiny bar. I leaned forward.

"Richie, is that you?"

It was a week since we'd seen him. He hadn't called round once while Johnny had been on leave. "Hello," he said.

At that moment Johnny came in with a beer in one hand and a lemonade shandy in the other. "Bunny's having a farewell drink with a couple of pals through there," he said, and then saw Richie. "Where have you been hiding yourself?"

"You don't want me around while you're enjoying your leave," Richie said. "Reminding you how real and earnest life can be outside. A specter at the feast—and that was never my style, children."

"Nonsense," I said. "Come to supper tonight."

"Yes, you must," Johnny said. "I want to hear what's going on. How are things?"

Which wasn't the kind of conversation I'd had in mind, but there wasn't much I could do to stop it. "Stettin last night," Richie told him. "A real stinkeroo. We lost five. I think there must have been half the Luftwaffe waiting for us over Holland on the way back. We were attacked by a whole flock of JU-88s in the same old place, west of Den Helder. Dixie Dean, my rear gunner, bought it. They've given me a new guy, a Canadian, just out of OTU." He shook his head and said bitterly, "I ask you. I've done eighty, Johnny. Eighty. Ten to go. What chance do I stand with a fresh kid like that in the tail? I went in to Cunningham. Really blew my stack."

"What did he have to say?"

"Told me he just didn't have anyone else at the moment. Things are bad, Johnny. We're losing a lot of good men. Hardly any of the old-timers around anymore."

A coldness touched me; icy fingers. I'd never heard

Richie speak quite like that before, panic in his voice. Johnny put a hand on his arm. "You need a break. If you're not on tomorrow why not have a day out? We could go down to Yarmouth or something like that."

"You could get some painting in," I said.

"That's a point." He grinned, looking more his usual self. "Mind if I bring Anne-Marie?"

"Why not?"

"Need a lift?" Johnny said.

Richie shook his head. "I'm on the bike. What time tonight?"

"Oh, around seven." Johnny leaned over the bar to call for cigarettes to the landlord in the public bar. I walked to the door with Richie. "Has it been really that bad, Richie?"

"I'll tell you something, Kate," he said. "This war just isn't funny anymore. See you at seven."

But we didn't, for he had an unexpected raid on Kiel, leaving at ten.

8

THE NEXT DAY he was on standby, although in the end they weren't called, and it was the same the day after. It was Wednesday before we got our day out.

My mother provided lunch in an old picnic basket we hadn't used for years. Johnny and I were in the MG and Richie and Anne-Marie followed on the motorbike, because I was supposed to know the way. We soon ran into trouble. Johnny didn't want to follow the main road down through Norwich and struck across country. As everywhere else in the English countryside at that time, all the signposts had been removed, and we were soon hopelessly lost.

Not that it mattered. It was a really beautiful day—the sun high, the sky very blue. Johnny stopped to ask the way twice, but there is a timeless quality about the Norfolk countryside. Little twisty lanes turning back on each other so that you find yourself mysteriously back at the same place you drove through twenty minutes before. It was rather like following one of those maze puzzles in a children's comic, trying one route after another, hoping to find your way by trial and error.

"At least Theseus had a ball of string," Johnny told me at one point. "All I have is you."

We came out into a road flanked by tall hedges, and in the distance, across a field of wheat, the sea sparkled. "There you are," I said, waving my hand.

He grinned. "Don't tell me you knew exactly where we were going all the time."

"Naturally."

A little further along the road, a farm gate stood open and a track stretched across the fields. We waited for Richie to catch up and Johnny called, "Let's see where this gets us."

The track was narrow and twisty. There were grass banks which had grown up over the centuries and after a while trees on either side, branches intertwining overhead to block the sun. We came out into an open section again and saw a man in the field on our left with a horse and cart.

Johnny braked to a halt. "I'll go and have words. See where we are."

He went through a gap in the hedge, and Richie pulled in behind and switched off his engine. It was very quiet, only the birds. I leaned my head back against the seat and watched a swallow high overhead.

I could hear laughter, then footsteps, and Richie leaned over me. "What are you dreaming about?"

I smiled up at him. "The usual stupidity. Wishing time could stand still. That this would never end."

He said gravely, "But life isn't like that, is it, Kate? We do the best with what we have." He shrugged. "After all, we seldom get what we'd really like, any of us, even in piping times of peace."

He was being serious and I didn't know why. Didn't really understand what he meant, not then, although later it became so terribly clear. In any case, we didn't get a chance to take it further because Johnny reappeared through the hedge.

"We're in luck. He says there's a good beach further along. No mines, just barbed wire, but there's a path through. Uses it himself."

"Fine," Richie said. "Let's get moving."

The track dropped down through trees and we emerged quite quickly into an area of sand dunes, barbed wire strung across them, the beach and that sparkling blue sea beyond. There was a headland about a quarter of a mile to our left, but not a single house in sight.

Johnny got out of the car. "This is it, folks," he called as Richie drove up. "All out"—and he gave me a hand over the door. The track went down through the dunes to where someone had cut the barbed wire, making a gap just wide enough to get through. Anne-Marie and I led the way and Johnny and Richie followed with the rugs and picnic basket. They dropped everything in a convenient spot. Johnny stood, hands on hips, looking at the sea.

"Perfect. This place probably hasn't seen a holiday-maker since the war started."

Richie said to Anne-Marie, "Come on, honey, let's take a look around."

They wandered off, following the line of sand dunes to the right. Johnny said, "Feel like a walk?"

"Why not?"

I took off my shoes and socks, rolled up my slacks and went down to the water's edge. "Aren't you coming in too?"

He shook his head. "No, thanks, but you play mermaid as much as you like."

We worked our way along the beach towards the head-land and I kept to the shallows all the way, Johnny hopping about to keep from getting his feet wet as the waves rushed in and out. He looked relaxed and completely at ease, skimming stones over the water like a small boy. As for me, I don't think I'd ever been so happy. The sun and sea, the complete solitude—and Johnny, of course.

I came out of the water to join him as we neared the end of the beach. "This is marvelous, isn't it?"

He smiled. "Like being the only two people left in the world." We had reached the headland, and a steep path climbed up from the beach above us. "You stay here," he said. "Too rough for bare feet. I'll see what the view's like."

I flung myself down in the sand and watched him climb. After a while I closed my eyes and just lay there, enjoying the warmth of the sun. A stone rattled. I opened my eyes again as he scrambled down the last few feet to join me.

He was laughing. "You're never going to believe this, but there's a village on the other side. Quite a large one." He smiled down. "That's life for you. You just never know what's on the other side of the hill."

The sun was very warm now. I stared up at him lazily and his face seemed to blur. Quite suddenly, he dropped to his knees, leaned down and kissed me. My experience in that direction was absolutely nil, but that didn't matter one little bit. I put my arms around his neck and held him tight. He pulled away quickly, something close to anger on his face. Not with me, I think, but with himself.

I sat up. "What is it? What's wrong?"

"Oh, no, Kate. Not that. Not with you."

"Why not?" I said. "I'm in love with you—or are you the only one around who doesn't realize that?"

He shook his head. "I don't have the right, can't you see that? Now let's get back to the others."

I scrambled to my feet. "But Johnny . . ."

"I told you once before to find someone with a future. You should have listened."

He turned and walked back along the beach quickly.

We put up a show for the sake of the other two, for Anne-Marie had unpacked the picnic basket and laid everything out on one of the rugs. Richie knew something was wrong, I could tell. His eyes kept flickering towards me curiously as we ate.

"There's booze cooling off in the pool over there," he told Johnny.

Johnny returned with a bottle of Chablis dripping water. "Where on earth did you get this?" he asked. "It's like gold these days."

"You know how it is. We wicked Yanks have our ways." Richie threw him a corkscrew.

Johnny opened it and passed Richie the bottle, and he poured wine into four plastic cups. I had moved a yard or two away to sit in the shade of a large rock to eat my sandwiches, and he brought mine over to me. "Half a cup —that's all you get. Goes to your head in this heat when you're not used to it."

"For goodness' sake, stop treating me like a child," I said. I was cross and it showed.

He squatted beside me. "What's wrong, kid?"

"Nothing, Richie. I've got a headache, that's all. I'd like to be on my own for a while."

He got up reluctantly and returned to the others. I drank some of the Chablis. It was deliciously cool, in spite of the plastic cup. To this day it has remained my favorite wine. The sun was hot, so very hot. I closed my eyes, my mind in a turmoil. I don't know what was going on. They were laughing and then the laughter started to fade. I could only hear the sea, and then that faded also and there was nothing.

I returned to life to find Johnny kneeling beside me. "You all right?"

I nodded. "Fine. What's happening?"

"Richie and I thought we'd take a run into the village. I need some cigarettes."

I'd thought he was almost out of the habit, for he had smoked only very occasionally during his leave. "Can't you manage?"

"I want to see if I can pick up some kind of present for your parents, anyway. It's been nice of them to put me up."

I closed my eyes again as he walked away. A couple of minutes later the engine of the MG burst into noisy life. After a while, I pushed myself up on one elbow. Anne-Marie sat on the rug, watching me.

She smiled, "How do you feel?"

"Fine. Didn't you want to see the village?"

"Too lazy and I'm enjoying this too much. This—this freedom. It's wonderful." She leaned back and closed her eyes, turning her face up to the sun.

I don't think we'd ever had a real conversation and I knew very little about her. I said, "Which part of Belgium are you from?"

"Brussels. My father was a radio producer on the news service there."

"What was it like?"

"When the Germans came?" She shrugged. "Not so bad at first. There was what you might call a honeymoon period, but then the Resistance started to operate and things got much tougher. Most people just did as they were told and got on with their daily lives. A smaller proportion collaborated. My father didn't like that and said so on one of his programs." She picked up a handful of sand and allowed it to trickle between her fingers. "He was the kind of man who always believed in saying what he thought."

I felt a chill. "Was?" I said.

"They came for him one night—the Gestapo, and the

Belgian police who were working with them. Took him away in a large black Mercedes." Her voice was very calm, very matter-of-fact. "That was the last I saw of him."

"And your mother?"

"Oh, she died before the war, so I was on my own. There didn't seem much point in staying, and a cousin of mine who was with the Resistance arranged for me to come out through Holland on one of the escape lines. I arrived in England last December." She smiled tightly. "Just in time for Christmas."

"And joined the WAAF?"

"That's right."

"And your father?"

"Who knows?"

She lay back on the rug, hands behind her head, and closed her eyes. I sat there, ashamed of the safe, enclosed life I had been leading while out there, across the water, thousands suffered under Nazi domination. It could so easily have happened to us if it hadn't been for Fighter Command and the English Channel. And what was I doing? What part was I playing in the grand scheme of things? I got up, suddenly restless, and went down towards the water's edge.

I walked along in the shallows for quite some distance, immersed in thought. After a while, I heard engines and looked up to see planes very high in the sky moving out to sea.

"Flying Forts," Johnny's voice said. "The Yanks having another go." I turned and found him on the beach a few yards away. "God knows how they do it. Deep-penetration raids in daylight are as good a way of committing suicide as I can imagine."

It was the last thing I wanted to think about. Anne-

Marie's story and now this, bringing back reality, the cold, harsh facts of life crowding out the sun. I didn't say anything. Just started to walk back, keeping to the shallows, and he kept pace with me.

There were hundreds of pebbles underfoot now. The sun, gleaming on them in the water, made them look deceptively pretty, with unusual designs. When I stopped to pick some up, they changed immediately, became smooth and faded. Strange how disappointed I felt, and Johnny obviously sensed it.

"What's real and what isn't?" he said. "It's often hard to tell, but that's life for you." He leaned down and picked something up. "This is more like it."

It was a large piece of green bottle glass, smoothed and rounded by the sea until it resembled a clear stone. "Make you a good paperweight."

I stood there looking down at it, the sea swirling round my ankles. He said softly, "I'm sorry, Kate. Sorry for upsetting you. I meant well."

"I know, Johnny." Suddenly I felt about a thousand years old. I reached out and touched his cheek. "It's going to be all right, I promise you."

His face was serious. He wanted to believe me, I realized that, but was unable to keep that black ironic humor of his from breaking through to the surface. "Who are you, then? The Old Woman of the Sea who knows all things?"

"Of course." I held up the green glass so that the sun filled it with light. "And this is my magic stone, the source of all my power. Hold it fast. Keep it with you at all times and nothing can harm you."

I placed it in the palm of his left hand and closed the fingers. He stared down at it, serious again, and managed to smile only with difficulty. "I could almost believe you."

"You must," I said. "Completely. That's the real secret.

The only one." I kissed him on the cheek, he took my hand and we started back along the shore.

Richie was sketching Anne-Marie when we got back. I looked over his shoulder. It was really very good. An excellent likeness. "I didn't know you could do that sort of thing."

"Lots of things you don't know about me." He finished the sketch in a few brief strokes, signed it and passed it across to her. Then he looked up at me. "Now your turn."

Anne-Marie moved out of the way and joined Johnny, who had dropped into the shade of a rock. I sat on the rug. Richie said, "Just lean back, hands behind you, look out to sea and keep quiet."

"Is this all right?" I inquired.

"Shut up!" he said.

It had been a wonderful day, but everything has to come to an end sometime, a lesson I had learned with some bitterness recently. Anne-Marie, Richie, Johnny and me—what was going to happen to us all? What would the end be? I had a tremendous desire to know, had a strange, weird feeling that if I concentrated just a little harder, all things would be revealed to me, and I drew back at the last moment, afraid.

I stayed there in a kind of limbo, my arms no longer hurting. Finally, Richie grunted and said, "That does it."

He passed it across. It was only a sketch, true, but quite marvelous. *Is that me*? I thought. *Can that really be me*? I turned to thank him and saw that he was just finishing off another.

"What's that?"

"Artist's copy. Rule of the house. This one's for me. Something to remember you by."

"That's very sweet," I said. "Thank you, Richie." I leaned over and kissed him on the cheek. Johnny and

Anne-Marie were down at the water's edge. I stood up. "I must show it to Johnny."

Richie's face darkened, the smile vanished instantly, but only for a moment. "Sure," he said. "Why not?" He glanced at his watch. "Time we were moving. I'll take the things up to the car while you get them."

He picked up the picnic basket and rugs and walked away and I watched him go, confused because in some way I'd hurt him and I didn't know how.

It was late evening as we came over the hill and drove down to the village. The rooks lifted out of the beech trees on either side of the lane, disturbed by our passing. I said, "They come from Russia—did you know that?"

"You're kidding," Johnny said.

"No, it's true."

He grinned. "You learn something new every day." He reached out to hold my hand for a moment. "Have you enjoyed it?"

"A day to remember," I said. "Perfection. Only everything has to come to an end sometime, doesn't it?"

He nodded. "That's about the size of it."

"Have you got your stone?"

He reached under the seat, driving with one hand, and produced the bubble of smooth green glass. "Wouldn't be without it."

"Good." I leaned back against the seat and closed my eyes, suddenly very tired.

9

Press on regardless was a current popular phrase, and that is exactly what everyone did. There was no other choice. Bunny O'Hara was given a brand-new Lancaster when he returned from fourteen days' sick leave. Not a patch on *Big Bertha*, he used to say. Officially it was *P for Peter*, but he soon had *Dark Rosaleen* painted on the nose. I was on duty at the canteen on the afternoon she was delivered, and we were all surprised when the Air Transport Auxiliary pilot emerged and turned out to be a woman. But then, women had to turn their hand to many jobs as strange in those dark days.

The day after *Big Bertha's* tragic end, the squadron had lost another kite, *Mary Anne*, badly shot up on the way home from a daylight raid on Kiel. It was only her second operation, and the crew had to bail out over Lincolnshire. The pilot, a flying officer called Swanson, having broken both legs landing on a concrete road, was out of the action. Bunny was offered the crew as a unit. He accepted on condition that he got Johnny as rear gunner. As the squadron leader raised no difficulties about that, it was all arranged.

I was at the canteen the first time they all met up at dispersal to go and look over *Dark Rosaleen*. It was strange how young they looked standing in a semicircle in front of Bunny and Johnny—like schoolboys in the headmaster's study. They even had their hands behind their backs. More boys for the slaughterhouse of Europe. Before the war ended, forty-seven thousand aircrew were to die—a fifty-percent casualty rate, and that was Bomber Command alone. It didn't give them much of a chance.

It was a bad time by night and day. On the seventeenth of August the American Eighth Air Force had launched a massive daylight attack on Schweinfurt and Regensburg. Three hundred and sixty-three B-17s set out. The cost in planes shot down or damaged beyond immediate repair was one hundred and eighteen. A third of the entire force. No one could stand losses like that for long.

As Richie pointed out, the truth was that the Germans were becoming too damned good, especially their night fighters, and their organization of tactics to combat Bomber Command's night raids was excellent.

So the slaughter went on. Heavier and heavier casualties during the next few weeks. I began to notice that even more faces were absent, although sometimes men were not around long enough for me to get to know them at all. I can remember Johnny introducing me to one crew, all new boys going out on their first operation. Two hours later they were dead, their kite exploded in midair over Holland after being attacked by three JU-88s. When I tried to recall what they'd looked like, I couldn't for the life of me remember.

Anne-Marie had been promoted to sergeant and posted to another station, which was the way things went in wartime, and Richie was very much at a loose end. He still came to the rectory, usually with Johnny, who continued to work on the manuscript of the *Rhapsody*, for which he had big plans. Nothing less than the Albert Hall, backed by the Hallé, and afterwards America—Carnegie Hall, the Hollywood Bowl.

"They'll love that uniform, kid," Richie assured Johnny.

Not that Johnny took him very seriously. In any case, he was still far from satisfied with the *Rhapsody*. The elusive something was still missing, hovering in the air just beyond his grasp.

Richie loved to talk to my father, and not just about flying in the First World War. He started turning up at Sunday services regularly and would come round to argue the point afterwards. Life, death, good and evil. He and my father had some wonderful rows. There was more to his constant visits than that, of course, although I was too naive to see it at the time.

Sitting in the conservatory listening to Johnny play, I'd be aware out of the corner of my eye of Richie watching me—always watching, a strange, rather sad expression on his face. It didn't make me feel uncomfortable. I generally turned to smile at him, and he would smile back. That Richie—handsome, dashing Captain Henri Richaud, the man most guaranteed to turn the head of every female for miles around—could possibly be in love with me simply never entered my foolish young head.

And then, one night just before a raid, I heard the sound of the motorbike in the drive outside. I wasn't due up at the canteen for another couple of hours, and I went to open the front door in surprise. Richie was sitting astride the bike, one knee up, smoking a cigarette, staring into the evening. He didn't even move as I went down the steps.

"Richie?" I said. "Is anything wrong?"

He started, turned and looked at me, face somber, then

smiled. "Not a thing, kid. I've got something for you, that's all."

He took a folder from the sidecar, opened it and produced a painting. It was the watercolor he had been working on the day he had taken me up to the airfield for the first time. The day which, as I see now, changed the course of my entire life.

It was so beautiful it hurt. The marsh, that incredible sky, the old mill, a curlew lifting from the reeds. There were tears in my eyes, I couldn't help them, as I looked up to thank him. "Richie, it's marvelous. What can I say?"

He shrugged. "I meant to give it to you some time ago, but forgot. Found it today when I was clearing out my room."

I frowned. "You're not going anywhere, are you?"

"No—no, of course not. Just putting things in order. You know how it is."

My heart moved inside me. I knew only too well what it meant when a flier started to talk like that. It meant that he had a premonition or, as Richie himself had often described it, he didn't feel too good. That kind of mood could be fatal. We were all worried enough about Richie as it was, for he had eighty-three ops in his logbook now. Only seven to go, and the entire Group held its collective breath, willing him to make it.

"What's wrong, Richie? What is it?"

He managed to look surprised. "Wrong? With me?" He zipped up his black leather flying jacket and started to pull on his gloves. "You think I've got the chop look or something?"

He swung a leg over the seat and stamped on the starter. "Richie?" It was a half-scream, drowned by the engine's roar.

I reached out, catching him by the sleeve. And then he did a strange thing. He turned my hand over and kissed the palm fiercely. When he looked up, his face was pale, his mouth opening and closing as if he wanted to speak, but couldn't find the right words.

He roared away, scattering gravel. I called his name—too late. I knew then, of course, what I had been too blind to see before. When I turned and went back up the steps, I was crying.

He received a bar to his DSO two days later for "brilliant leadership and distinguished and gallant conduct under fire," although the citation had a great deal more to say than that. The one disturbing note was an unfortunate incident at the George, where we had all gone for a celebratory drink. Richie was approached by a rather unpleasant flight lieutenant called Bulliver who'd obviously had more to drink than was good for him. On top of that, he didn't like Americans and had often said so.

"They might have waited until you finished the tour, Richaud," he said.

Richie smiled amiably. "You know how it is, *old man.*" He rather overstressed that bit. "They're not sure that I will, and the English, being sentimentalists at heart, didn't want to disappoint me."

It was a terrible thing to say, and everyone stopped talking abruptly. Bulliver was thrown. He looked around him uncertainly, then reached forward and picked at the silver rose on Richie's DSO ribbon that meant a second award. "I must say that it seems to be taking the special relationship just a little too far. Lend-lease, I suppose?"

Richie smiled faintly, and it was Johnny who said, "You wouldn't know the real thing if it was stuck under your nose, Bulliver."

Bulliver rounded on him. "How dare you speak to me like that? I'll have you on a charge before you know what's hit you, Stewart."

Bunny O'Hara took a hand. There was an empty bottle on the bar. He picked it up and advanced on Bulliver, and there was murder in his eyes. "Get out!" he said very softly. "Get out or I'll smash your face in."

He added something in Irish which I certainly didn't understand and neither did Bulliver, but he went quickly enough and there was no question of any charges later.

Two nights later I was lying in a deck chair in the garden, watching the sun go down on the far side of the hill, when I heard the MG turn in at the gate. A moment or so later Johnny and Richie came round the side of the house.

"There you are," Johnny said.

They crossed the lawn and Richie flopped down into the deck chair beside me. "Is that lemonade in the jug? Great. Don't think I'll ever move again."

"And what are you two up to?" I demanded. There was something going on, I could tell.

Johnny ignored my question. "Your mother and father in?"

"In the living room. Waiting for *ITMA* to start on the wireless. I wouldn't interrupt, if I were you. My father won't even accept telephone calls when Tommy Handley is on."

"We'll see." Johnny walked across the lawn and went in through the French windows.

"What on earth is going on?" I asked, and started to get up.

"Take it easy." Richie pulled me down. "He just wants to find out if they're free for the day on Monday. You too."

"Free?" I asked. "On Monday?" By now, of course, I was completely bewildered. "I don't understand."

He lit a cigarette and leaned back in the deck chair. "It's really very simple. Johnny and I have a rather special appointment in London, Monday morning. We're allowed a couple of guests each. As neither of us has anyone close we could ask to a thing like this, we thought we'd make do with you and your parents between us."

"Appointment?" I said.

"That's right. At Buckingham Palace."

We all went down by train overnight Sunday, changing at Peterborough to the main-line express. Not that in those days it was particularly fast; conditions were so bad that you were glad to get there at all. The station was dingy and depressing, all the windows painted black, plastered with notices demanding to know whether your journey was really necessary and warning that walls had ears. The train was so crowded that we spent most of the journey in the corridor. I must say everyone seemed incredibly cheerful about it. But then, in those days, we were all in the same boat.

There was a raid on London that night—nothing very much, but we were halted on the track outside for more than three hours before they would let us come into King's Cross station. By then it was just after ten, and the boys were due at the palace at eleven, which didn't leave us much time. Richie left us waiting at the main entrance and by some mysterious wizardry known only to the American serviceman returned with a taxi ten minutes later.

The driver was suitably impressed when my father gave him our destination and lost no time in getting us there. It started raining as we turned into the Mall. Richie said, "Last time I was here it was bright sunshine, a really beautiful afternoon. The ceremony was held in the courtyard with the band of the Grenadier Guards playing."

I said to my father, "What about you, Daddy? Did the old King give you your medal?"

He shook his head. "I was still in hospital in France. Some general or other handled it."

We rounded Victoria's monument and were checked at the main gate, where the taxi was allowed through to drop us in the inside courtyard. The driver refused his fare and drove away as my father tried to argue with him.

Richie and Johnny left us at the main entrance, and we followed the crowd up the red-carpeted stairs to the long picture gallery, where there were rows and rows of gold chairs facing the central dais, with its fluted columns on either side, where the King would stand. A Guards' band —I was told later it was the Blues—played waltzes and excerpts from light opera as we waited.

I found the whole thing quite fascinating. There were marble statues in niches, portraits of royal soldiers in scarlet tunics. As for the crowd, most of the women wore black, and there were a fair number of older folk, presumably mothers and fathers, and a few children. The thing which did surprise me was the fact that many people arrived late—in some cases a good twenty minutes after the official time laid down on the tickets.

The talking died away and there was a hush all around us. The band broke into the National Anthem and the King, dressed in naval uniform, walked through the doors which had been thrown open.

He took up his position on the dais flanked by several aides, all in uniform, and the investiture started with a minimum of fuss, the long line of recipients moving forward slowly. The Navy came first as the senior service, followed by the Army, with the RAF last in line. And they had all been formed up according to order of decorations.

As each man's name was called out, followed by his ship or unit, he went forward, and it was interesting that no details of the deed behind the award were given.

Eight RAF officers received the DSO that morning. Richie, conspicuous in American uniform, was the last to go up. The King pinned the cross of the order to his chest, and they spoke for a few moments and he laughed at something Richie said to him.

Johnny was next in line, the only recipient of the CGM that morning. I was so proud of him as he went forward that my stomach cramped, and I leaned over slightly, clenching the black patent handbag my mother had lent me tightly between my hands. I wanted the moment to be just right. Something he could hold on to. Remember for the rest of his life. *The rest of his life.* With twelve ops to go? A wave of grayness passed over me, and I pushed the thought firmly away and concentrated on *now*.

The King pinned the medal on his chest, smiling briefly, and spoke to him. Johnny told me later that he'd asked him how his hands were. He'd actually remembered the details of the DFM award after all this time. They seemed to have quite a conversation, and then the King bowed slightly, as he had done to everyone: a tribute to their courage, I suppose; thanking them on behalf of all of us.

My father turned to smile at me, reaching for my hand. I'm sure he was well aware of how much that moment meant. He was always extraordinarily perceptive. "You must be proud of him," he said.

It was only then that I allowed myself to cry a little, and not for long.

My father insisted on taking us all out for an early lunch. The Café Royale, no less. By wartime standards it was a splendid meal. Afterwards, he and my mother left us to visit an old colleague of his who was on the staff at St. Paul's, after agreeing to meet us at King's Cross in time to catch the eight-thirty for Peterborough that evening.

There was still time to hear the second half of the lunchtime concert at the Royal Exchange. Richie wanted some more exciting fare and took himself off to the Nuffield Centre, arranging to meet us there later.

When we reached the Exchange the concert room was packed, which wasn't surprising, for Myra Hess was playing. We had to stand, and Johnny leaned against a pillar, listening intently, giving her all his attention. As I recall, the program was mainly Bach, although she ended with a strange little piece called "Le Pastour" by Gabriel Grovlez, which she played with extraordinary feeling.

And Johnny, as we made our way out through the crowd, had a kind of sadness on his face. "What's wrong?" I asked him.

"Oh, I'm just feeling sorry for myself."

"Why?"

"Because I'll never be as good as that—not now." He held out his hands for a moment, the burn grafts stretched tight, the shiny skin gleaming dully. "And I could have been, Kate." I caught him by the sleeve as he started to move on and pulled him round to face me. "Only now you never can be, that's a fact of life. So what do you intend to do about it?"

"Dance the feet off you all afternoon." He grabbed my arm and hurried me away through the crowd.

The Nuffield Centre was in Wardour Street, a club offering free entertainment to servicemen. Most of the famous stars of the day appeared there from time to time.

It was all very exciting to me, for I'd never been to such a place. Roy Fox and his band were appearing that afternoon, and the place was packed with servicemen of every kind—French, Poles, Belgians, Americans and, of course, British, plus masses of girls. Almost the first thing we saw when we went in was Richie dancing cheek to cheek with a blond ATS corporal. We moved into the throng and joined them.

I was in Johnny's arms; the lights were low; that wonderful band was playing. I was closer to heaven than I had ever dreamed possible. Somehow I just didn't seem to get tired, and we danced the whole of the afternoon.

But the most poignant moment came later on, during an interval when we continued to dance to records. They played one I will always remember. Al Bowly, who'd been killed in the London blitz, singing "A Foggy Day in London Town." It reminded me of that first night I was with Johnny—the dance at the village hall. I leaned my head against his shoulder as we circled in the half-light and wished that it could go on forever.

We left soon after that, having had a brief word with Richie, who arranged to meet us at seven on the steps of the Victoria monument in front of Buckingham Palace. "But we've just been there," Johnny said. "What's the big idea?"

"Just thought I'd like to see the old place again before I go," Richie told him, "and it seems like a good idea to me to end the day where it began."

Which made a certain kind of uneasy sense. But then, I told myself that perhaps I was looking too much for undercurrents in Richie's words these days.

Strangely enough, it *was* foggy that evening in spite of the time of year. I can remember walking along the Embankment with Johnny at six o'clock, foghorns hooting mournfully out there in the Pool of London. Traffic sounds were muted and far away, so that even the lapping of the water along the Embankment against the wall below seemed louder. It was quiet and still, and we hardly exchanged a word.

We went along in a silence that went on and on. It was a moment when everything I felt for Johnny welled up inside me until my eyes were full of tears. I stared blindly into the fog, our shoulders touching. The sense of his presence almost overwhelmed me. When he put his arms around me and kissed me it seemed the most natural thing in the world.

We walked on in silence, all the way up the Mall until finally we were back in front of the palace. And Richie was right. It *did* seem a fitting way to end the day.

Johnny stood on the steps of the monument lighting a cigarette, then looked up at Queen Victoria. "I wonder what the old girl thinks of all this."

He turned suddenly as if aware that I was watching him.

"It's going to be all right, Johnny. It's going to be fine."

He smiled beautifully. "Of course it is. I feel great. Never better."

But the eyes weren't smiling. My stomach went hollow, and for no accountable reason I knew what they meant about premonitions.

A horn sounded and a taxi swerved in to the curb, Richie hanging out of the window. "In you get, children," he called. "Play's over for today. Back to the sweatshop."

I sat in the rear, sandwiched between him and Johnny, feeling very depressed indeed. Richie kept up a barrage of his usual nonsense, but neither Johnny nor I said a word. When we got out of the taxi at King's Cross, Johnny went on ahead to look for my mother and father. Richie paid the cabby, then turned to me.

"Anything wrong?"

I shook my head. "I'm a bit depressed at the thought of going back to it, that's all."

He put an arm around my waist and kissed me on the

cheek. "Cheer up, kid. Some stories do have happy endings, even in real life."

But how could I believe that when Johnny, as I was
painfully aware, still had twelve ops to go?

10

THINGS WEREN'T THE SAME after that. During the week
that followed, Johnny went out twice—Essen and
Hamburg; but something had happened to him. He grew
increasingly morose and bitter. He still came to the rectory, spent hours at the Bechstein working away at the
Rhapsody, which wasn't going well at all. That elusive
something that he sought for so hard still stayed tantaliz-
ingly just out of his reach.

Perhaps that was the reason. Certainly there seemed to
be a barrier between us, and things came to a head towards the end of the following week when there was a
big raid on Genoa. *Dark Rosaleen* was scratched at the
eleventh hour because of some engine fault or other that
they couldn't locate, but Richie went in *Jenny Gone* and
had a close call.

Genoa was a nine-hour trip in the best of conditions.
That night there was a sudden change of weather and
they ran into head winds on the way home which added
an additional hour's flying time. Six planes didn't make it
back at all. *Jenny Gone* was almost one of them, losing
her port outer engine over the North Sea. But Richie, bril-

liant as ever, nursed her to the Lincolnshire coast and managed to put down at a station called Brigg. He and the crew were returned to Upton Magna by truck, leaving *Jenny Gone* to have the faulty engine checked.

Most of this I got from my father. Richie hadn't been round for a few days, and Johnny never mentioned him. I wondered if they'd quarreled, but didn't like to ask because of the mood Johnny was in. Saturday morning, he came early and worked at the piano for three hours, virtually ignoring me, then announced that he was going for a walk on the marsh.

"I'll get my coat," I said.

He shook his head. "I'd like to be on my own for a while. I want to think."

"What's wrong, Johnny?" I asked. "We can't go on like this. It's just making things unbearable."

"Wrong?" he said. "Who in the hell said anything was wrong? It's simple enough. I just want to go out on my own for a while. I want to think this damned thing out. See where I'm going wrong. I can't do that with you sitting there staring at me all the time."

He walked out and the door slammed. There was silence, for I was alone in the house. I was furiously angry, pulled on my mac and went out myself.

It was raining slightly, a light drizzle, as I walked along the lane, hands pushed deep into my pockets, fists clenched. There was the sudden familiar roar of the motorbike's engine behind me and Richie pulled up alongside.

"Whither away, pretty maid?" He sat there astride the bike. "You look just a little bit cheesed off to me."

"You could say that."

"Trouble?"

I shrugged. "Oh, I don't know what's wrong with him these days, Richie. What's he like at the base?"

"Withdrawn," he said. "But I wouldn't worry too much. Everybody goes through these patches."

"I know one thing. I can't take much more of it."

He sat there for a moment, tapping his fingers on the handlebars thoughtfully. And then he grinned, that peculiarly Richie grin which meant he was up to no good. "What you need is a little action, and I think I've got just the answer. How would you feel about a trip in a Lancaster to cheer you up? Time you sampled the real thing."

I was startled, to put it mildly. "You must be joking."

"No, I'm serious. I'm leaving for Brigg in half an hour to bring back *Jenny Gone*. It's only a twenty-minute flight, but you could see what Lincoln Cathedral looks like from the air."

"It's against regulations," I said, aware of the excitement rising inside me.

"Of course it is, but nobody who counts need know a thing about it. I'm only taking Barney Henderson, my flight engineer, and Taff Hughes, the wireless op. The WAAF from the motor pool who's driving us up is a very particular friend of mine. She won't say a word to anyone. Hour and a half to get there, that's all. Come on—you'll be home again before you know it. There's your mother and father to consider, of course."

"They've gone to Norwich for the day."

"There you are, then. They don't need to know a thing about it. What about the laughing boy?"

"Walking on the marsh."

"That gets rid of him. He probably wouldn't think much of the idea anyway."

Which, needless to say, made me absolutely determined to go. But there was more to it than that. It was somehow a way of getting back at him—but for that to happen, it was essential that he know exactly what was going on.

"All right," I said, "as long as you take me back to the house first. I want to leave a note telling him where I've gone."

"Claws at last, Kate." He smiled softly. "Now, that *is* an interesting development. All right. Hop on behind and let's get moving."

I scrambled on to the pillion, far from elegant with my skirt up above my knees, and he drove back along the lane.

There was no trouble with Barney Henderson and Taff Hughes, who thought the whole thing a huge joke. The WAAF driver had eyes only for Richie, who flirted shamelessly with her all the way to Brigg. I'd changed into slacks, and they'd provided flying boots and jacket for me —far too big, of course—and I had a leather flying helmet with goggles. I stayed well back out of sight inside the truck behind Barney and Taff as we passed in through the main gate and moved on to the hangars.

It was the quiet period and there weren't too many people about. *Jenny Gone* was waiting close to the runway. The WAAF, on Richie's instructions, drove straight out to her, parking so that we were only a few yards away from the main hatch, which stood open.

For the moment, there was no one about. Richie said, "All right, boys, get her inside. Fast as you like. You haven't a thing to worry about, Kate. Everybody looks the same in that gear from a distance."

It had started to rain. As we scrambled over the tailboard I was aware of a jeep approaching from the left. "All right, girl, just keep on going," Taff said in that beautiful Welsh voice of his, and pushed me forward.

I reached the open hatch, and Barney gave me a shove up and inside as the jeep braked to a halt. I glanced back and saw a tall warrant officer with a bristling moustache get out. He saluted smartly.

"Keep moving," Barney whispered.

I clambered over the main spar and took the navigator's seat. Outside I could hear the warrant officer saying, "I think you'll find everything all right now, sir. Tested that engine myself this morning. Sure you want to go? Lousy met forecast. Cloud base moving down by the minute."

"Twenty-minute flight," Richie said cheerfully. "Not worth worrying about. Better get moving, though, before things get worse."

"Your funeral, sir," the warrant officer said. "I've already had the engines run up for you, so she's ready to go when you are."

Richie was inside a moment later, pulling the door shut after him. Taff was already at the radio set, and Barney was in the flight engineer's seat, checking the panel on the starboard side. Richie said briskly, "Right, Taff, contact tower for clearance. Tell them we're ready to leave."

He squeezed past Barney and strapped himself into the pilot's seat. I pulled myself up into the mid-upper turret, which gave the best all-round view in the plane. I got something of a shock, for several mechanics had appeared outside and were waiting, under the stern eye of the warrant officer, to pull the chocks away when Jenny was ready to go.

I strapped myself into the seat and pulled my goggles down, and Taff reached up to check that I'd done it properly. Richie called, "Let's test helmet intercoms."

They'd already instructed me about that during the journey in the truck. I plugged in my lead and waited. Richie's voice crackled in my ear. "Okay, Barney?"

"Okay, Skipper."

"Okay, Taff?"

Then he said, "How's the mid-upper gunner doing?"

I swallowed hard and flicked the switch as they'd instructed me. "Okay, Skipper."

The port outer engine roared into life. It seemed absolutely deafening, but the noise was as nothing compared with the sound when all four were turning over. It was so familiar. As if I'd been through all this before. The instruments, even the radio sets, were shaking. The whole aircraft seemed to vibrate.

The mechanics outside ran forward to pull the chocks away and there was a squeal of brakes as we lurched forward. The dialogue between Richie and Barney was constant. Much of it I understood, mainly because of all those drills Richie had taught me. I was so excited that somehow I managed to pull out the plug of my intercom and heard nothing of what came after.

We were moving now, taxiing past a long line of Lancasters towards the end of the main runway. We started to turn, then waited. The noise of the four Merlin engines seemed to rise to a shriek that drowned everything. We surged forward, gathering speed.

That was the strangest part of the whole thing—that I was unconscious of speed at all, only the runway turning beneath us endlessly. I could see trees in the far distance, rushing towards us, and then we seemed to lurch and the trees were below and receding. I turned to look back and saw Brigg airfield laid out behind me like a model of the real thing for children to play with. And then it was far away and there was only the flat Lincolnshire countryside beneath.

"Pilot to rear gunner. You had enough back there?"

I sat in the rear turret behind the guns, rain lashing against the Perspex, the countryside a thousand feet below wreathed in mist. So now I had the feel; now I knew what it was like. I clasped the handles of the guns gently and swung the turret from side to side.

Taff's voice crackled over the intercom. "This weather's going to get worse before it gets better, Skipper. Cloud dropping fast and more rain forecast."

"Not to worry," Richie replied. "Home before you know it. Just drop in on Lincoln Cathedral first."

"I think Taff's right, Skip; we should get out of this."

"Nonsense," Richie replied. "I made the lady a promise, and a Southern gentleman never goes back on his word."

We plunged into mist and the ground below simply disappeared. His voice crackled calmly in my ears again. "Let's shake this bloody lot. I'm going down."

My stomach was hollow with excitement and yet I can truthfully say that I wasn't afraid. I suppose I had too much faith in him for that, but I think what happened then shook even Richie.

We burst out of the mist at four hundred feet, still going down, and found the city of Lincoln spread out below us. Barney cried out, "Pull up! Pull her up, for Christ's sake!"

And then we were roaring across rooftops, and the Cathedral seemed to be coming up at a very steep angle. "There she is, kid," Richie said calmly, and banked to starboard, climbing hard.

I think that for a moment, I actually stopped breathing. Taff was almost sobbing as he said, "Only five to go, Skip. Five to go, remember."

Richie laughed. "You worry too much. Stick with me and you'll live forever."

Rain chased us all the way home, and at Upton Magna we were cleared for an immediate landing. Richie brought her in for a perfect touchdown. We taxied along to disperal and finally slowed to a halt. One by one, those great engines were switched off. The silence was uncanny —only the drumming of the rain on the roof, voices outside as the ground crew went into action.

I left the rear turret and went forward, and Richie met me halfway. "Well, how was it?"

"Memorable," I said.

He put his hands on my shoulders and grinned. "We must do it again. New Orleans next time."

Barney, who looked as if he had aged several years since we started, said, "What about Kate, Skipper?"

"You stay here for a minute. I'll go and bring the pickup truck in nice and close."

We could hear it drive up outside and brake sharply. Richie pushed the handles down and swung the hatch open. "Well, well," he said.

Johnny appeared in the opening, his face white. He looked so furiously angry that it frightened me. He glared up at Richie. "Wing Commander Cunningham wants you on the double. It might interest you to know that your stupid caper over Lincoln Cathedral's had the telephone wire burning for the past fifteen minutes. Everyone from the Chief Constable to the Bishop himself."

"That's encouraging," Richie said.

Johnny reached up and grabbed him by the front of his flying jacket. "Go to hell your own way, but you don't take her with you."

Richie's face went very dark. Johnny shoved him away, reached for my hand and pulled me out through the hatch so violently that I fell to one knee. The MG was parked a few yards away. For the moment, the few mechanics around were busy up front.

He gave me a push. "Get inside before I break your neck."

I got the flying jacket and helmet off before we reached

the main gate. As we turned into the road I said, "It wasn't Richie's fault. You've no right to think that."

"What are you trying to say? That it was your idea? Don't be stupid, Kate. It doesn't suit you."

We drove the rest of the way to the rectory in silence. He turned into the drive and braked to a halt at the bottom of the steps. It was only as I climbed over the door that I realized that I was still wearing flying boots. He burst into laughter.

"Have you any idea what you look like? They're about five sizes too big for you."

I reached out to him then, and he grabbed my hand and held it to his lips. "God, but I was frightened, Kate. Never again. Never anything like that. Promise me?"

I stroked his hair, holding him to me, at that moment closer to him than I had ever been.

It was the second week in September, autumn coming in fast. The weather broke with a vengeance. One gale after another, and almost constant rain. Operations were constantly canceled, which didn't go down well with the crews, who had to spend a great deal of time just sitting around in flying gear, waiting for fresh orders or a break in the weather.

I saw more of Johnny, of course. He seemed as withdrawn and morose as ever, although he made an obvious effort when he was with me. I think he was unhappy because of the situation between himself and Richie. Since the Lincoln Cathedral incident they hadn't been on speaking terms.

Richie stayed away from the rectory. In that he was only being diplomatic, and there seemed little point in simply inviting him to supper and presenting Johnny with a fait accompli. But I couldn't allow it to go on. They were having enough troubles without this, and it was, after all, my fault. But what to do about it?

In the end, as is often the way, it virtually solved itself. They were doing Genoa again on the night of the eighteenth. Another big one. Nine weary hours. All the way across Europe and back again. And this one was special. Richie's eighty-eighth. Two to go after this, and for Johnny, five.

I was on duty at the canteen that night. Would not have missed it for anything in life, not at that stage of the game. Departure was scheduled for eight o'clock and there was a last-minute delay of one hour.

We were suddenly busy, aircrew crowding around the counter for hot tea and sandwiches. I hadn't been feeling too good. A migraine sort of headache; I'd been getting them a lot lately and was glad to be busy. During a lull, I looked out over the crowd and saw Johnny standing alone smoking a cigarette, his parachute pack on the ground at his feet. Richie was standing nearby, looking elaborately the other way. The sheer stupidity of it made me so angry that I wanted to explode. Instead, I put two mugs of tea on a tray, went out and pushed my way through the crowd towards them.

"Tea, Sergeant?" I said to Johnny.

There was bewilderment on his face, but he reached for one of the mugs automatically. I held out the tray to Richie. "Captain?"

He turned slowly; looked at the tray, at me, then at Johnny. He smiled. "Why, thank you, ma'am," he said, thickening that Southern accent as only he could on occasion.

Johnny was smiling too, and I knew it was going to be all right. I had to fight to control my tears, dropped the tray and reached out for both of them. "Oh, you fools," I said. "Never, never do anything to me like that again."

The Tannoy crackled into life overhead, and suddenly everyone was on the move. "Got to go, Kate." Johnny brushed my cheek lightly, snatched up his parachute and was away.

"Kate." Richie was trying to say something to me, but there was so much noise that I couldn't hear what it was. His mouth was opening and closing, and as the crowd swept him away he vainly reached out a hand.

I felt terrible—a presentiment, perhaps? One thing was certain: I couldn't go on, for the migraine was so bad now that I could hardly stand. I lay down on the bunk in the caravan after the last plane had taken off, but it was no good. After a while, my mother arranged for one of the WAAFs from the motor pool to run us home in a jeep.

She put me to bed with warm milk, aspirins, a hot-water bottle. All the usual things. Left me to sleep it off and returned to the base with the jeep.

It was one of the worst nights I have ever spent. I twisted and turned, haunted by bad dreams, crying with the pain on occasion, finally falling asleep from sheer exhaustion sometime after midnight.

I came awake suddenly, the pale light of dawn filtering into the room. I lay there for a moment, staring up at the ceiling, aware that something was wrong, something was different. And then I heard it: music faintly, in the distance.

I was out of bed in a moment, grabbing for my dressing gown. I opened the door. The music was louder, much louder, drifting up the stairs from the conservatory. When I went down, the door stood open. Johnny was sitting at the Bechstein, the French windows open behind him. Rain drifted through, the curtain lifting in a slight breeze.

He still wore his flying jacket. His face was filthy, the marks of the goggles clearly defined. And his playing? It was like nothing I'd ever heard before—wild and beautiful, full of a tremendous driving force. The *Rhapsody* and yet not the *Rhapsody*.

I stood at one end of the piano. "Johnny?" I said.

He looked up, a savage smile on his face. "Another bloody butcher's shop. They were waiting for us all the way back. I think every night fighter in Germany and Holland was in the air tonight."

The heart turned cold inside me. I had difficulty in breathing. "All gone, Kate, all the old-timers. We're the only ones left, Bunny and me."

There was a new savage intensity in his playing, a deep, menacing rumble in the bass that I'd never heard before. "Hear that, Kate?" he said. "That's what was missing all the time. The sound of the bombers. The sound of the bloody bombers."

The playing rose to a crescendo, then stopped abruptly. He banged down the lid and lurched to his feet, and there were tears in his eyes. "Don't you realize what I'm trying to say?"

I spoke, but only with difficulty. "Richie?"

He fell across the piano, buried his face in his arms and wept.

I heard a car turn into the drive. A moment later the front door opened. As I turned, my father appeared in the hall. I put a finger to my lips, went out quickly and closed the conservatory door behind me.

"I came as soon as I heard the news," he said. "I looked for him everywhere at the airfield. When I checked at the gate, they told me he'd driven out in the MG. How is he?"

"Better let alone for the moment." I was astonished at

my own calm, my lack of tears. But those, of course, would come later. "What happened?"

He took off his cap wearily and led the way into the kitchen. "Your mother's still needed at the canteen. I said I'd go back for her in an hour." I put the kettle on and he sat down and filled his pipe. "A bad business. Six or seven planes gone as far as I can make out. They're hoping some of the crews are all right, of course. We already knew that one crash-landed safely on the Suffolk coast."

"And Richie?"

"Last heard of over the Dutch coast under heavy attack by night fighters. Someone thought they had radio contact with him twenty minutes later, but they could be mistaken. Nothing since."

I was filled with a fierce, wild hope. "They could be down in the sea, then. Or maybe they've made an emergency landing at one of the coastal stations. That sort of thing happens all the time. You know that."

"Perhaps." He reached out and took my hand. "But I wouldn't bank on it, Kathie."

I made the tea and gave him a cup, then took one in to Johnny. He still sat at the piano, smoking a cigarette, staring out at the rain. His shoulders were quivering, and when I gave him the tea the cup rattled in the saucer.

He smiled tightly. "A touch of the shakes, that's all. I've had it before. Soon goes." He closed his eyes. "My head's splitting. All I can smell is Lancaster. I need some fresh air."

"Do you want to go for a walk?"

He opened his eyes and nodded almost eagerly. "Yes, I think I'd like that more than anything else on earth at this moment, Kate."

We went out along the dike. He didn't speak a word, and for the life of me I couldn't think of anything to say. There was rain coming in off the sea on a light wind. The grass was slippery with it. Once, I slipped, almost falling. He caught me automatically.

"Thanks," I said, but it was as if he hadn't heard.

The tide was out, much further than I had ever seen it. When we reached the end of the first dike, we could see vast areas of wet sand stretching into the mist and occasionally, when the wind tore a gap in the curtain, great banks lifting out of the sea in the distance.

We paused and Johnny lit a cigarette. "Is it safe to go out there?"

"At this stage of the tide, yes."

He walked down the bank without another word and started across the sand, and I went after him. I almost had to run to keep up with him and held on to his arm, desperate for something to say. And at the end, I had to make it the wrong thing.

"Johnny?"

He didn't even bother to look at me. "What?"

"Have you still got your magic stone?"

He stopped abruptly, turned and glared at me. He pushed me away violently and felt in one of the pockets of his flying jacket. The stone seemed to glow with green fire in the gray morning.

"There's your damned stone!" he said. "If you want it, you'll have to fish for it!"

He threw it away from him; it bounced once, then disappeared beneath the surface of a pool. He started to turn. I grabbed his arm. "Johnny, please . . ."

His fingers hooked into me; his face was a stranger's face. Quite suddenly, the wind ripped away the mist behind him and I saw the tail plane of a Lancaster sticking out of the water several hundred yards away. My mouth opened, but I could not speak. I pointed. Johnny turned to look. His grip on me slackened, and then he was running.

Most of the plane was underwater. The main hatch was open just below the surface, and the mid-upper turret stood clear. Johnny pulled off his boots. "Stay back!" he called, and floundered into the water towards the hatch.

I didn't hesitate for a moment. I've always been an exceptionally strong swimmer, but in any case my right now was as great as his. Nothing on this earth could have made me stay back. I pulled off my Wellingtons, waded into the water and swam towards the port wing, which was steeply inclined and perhaps three feet below the surface.

The water must have been intensely cold, but I wasn't aware of that fact as I worked my way along, half wading, my feet feeling for balance on that slippery wing.

The water was like black glass, clearer than anything I have known. I could see the painted bombs, the DSO, the legend *Jenny Gone*; and there was the cockpit, Perspex still intact. I took a deep breath and pulled myself down, reaching for the edge.

Richie was in there, seated at the controls, strapped into the pilot's seat. His eyes were still open, a faint smile on his lips as if he were pleased to see me. The spotted scarf he always wore danced around his neck. His arms floated in the water, reaching out to me.

11

JOHNNY HAD TWO TRIPS in quick succession on Thursday and Friday. On Saturday they buried Richie at St. Peter's in accordance with the instructions contained in a letter discovered amongst his effects.

It was a bright, crisp morning, a light breeze rustling in the leaves of the beech trees overhead, the rooks calling to each other. A scattering of cirrus clouds very high in a sky of deepest blue. *Good flying weather*. It was going to be hot later on.

There was quite a crowd. Not only friends from the squadron, but all the top brass, as Richie would have called them, from Group. There were also a Brigadier General Harvey of the USAAF base at Thuxtead, ten miles up the road, and a Major Parker, a B-17 bomber pilot, who didn't look much older than Richie. And the firing squad was half American, half British.

The coffin was draped with a Stars and Stripes flag. I stood on one side with my mother. We wore black, of course, because it was the correct thing to do. I stood there in borrowed coat and hat, clutching the ugly black patent handbag. I was devoid of all feeling, completely numb as I had been from the moment we'd found him.

The officers from Group stood opposite, and Johnny was a little to one side on his own. He was in his best uniform and, like everyone else, wore his medals. His face was pale, dark circles under the eyes, and he seemed tired. Berlin the night before. *Eight hours.* He didn't look across at me at all; simply stared down at the coffin, hands folded in front of him.

My father stood at the head, his medals pinned to his robes. I remember how the sun gleamed on them as he spoke out in a high, brave voice. *I am the resurrection and the life, saith the Lord; he that believeth in me, though he were dead, yet shall he live. . . .*

The Book of Common Prayer contains some of the most beautiful words in the English language, but for me they were totally meaningless that morning, devoid of all sentiment. No comfort there at all. They washed over me like the tide sweeping in across the marsh. My eyes were hot. Burning. I could not weep. There was a shouted command; the rifles volleyed; the rooks rose in alarm, crying angrily.

The flag was taken from the coffin, folded neatly and passed to Major Parker, who handed it to General Harvey. The coffin was lowered. Suddenly the words changed, became intelligible again. What my father, in his infinite wisdom, was saying was for me, I think, as much as for Richie.

> *I was ever a fighter so—one fight more,*
> * the best and the last!*
> *I would hate that Death bandaged my eyes*
> * and forbore*
> *And bade me creep past.*

Major Parker was beside me, saluting, and I saw that he too wore RAF wings above his right tunic pocket.

After a moment of silence, the Major turned to me and said quietly, "General Harvey would appreciate it if he could have a word with you."

I stared at him, dazed, and he moved to one side and the General stepped forward. He held the Stars and Stripes which had draped the coffin in his two hands. "Miss Hamilton," he said, "it's our custom, in such tragic circumstances, to give this to the next of kin. In a letter found among his effects, Captain Richaud stipulated that it was to go to no one else but you."

I took the flag from him, as in a dream, and he stepped back and saluted. "A fine officer, ma'am. A brave gentleman."

I stood there holding the flag in my hands, staring across the open grave at Johnny. Now he was looking at me, too. His eyes were very dark; he seemed to look through me, far, far out to sea. Suddenly, he turned and walked away through the gravestones, and something clicked. I was no longer in a dream, for this was real, this was happening—and Richie was dead.

There was no sign of Johnny when we got back to the rectory, but by then I was in a high fever and my mother insisted on putting me to bed and calling the doctor. I fought against it, but without success. "I won't go to bed," I said. "Must go to the canteen tonight. Johnny might be on."

It was my father who settled that for me, brutally and directly—the best possible way. "He's on now, Kate. Do you understand? A daylight raid on Kiel. That's why he left so abruptly. He didn't have time to hang about."

I fainted after that, must have done, because the next thing I remember is old Dr. Soames sitting on the edge of the bed with a stethoscope round his neck, checking me over. My mother was there too. From what he was saying to her, I got the impression that he didn't think that early-morning swim when we'd found Richie had done me any good. He held a glass to my lips. I don't know what was in it, but everything receded, simply slipped away. My eyes closed.

When I opened them again, it was early evening and Johnny was standing at the window smoking a cigarette and staring out into the garden.

I made some sort of movement. He turned, came over at once and sat on the edge of the bed. "You had us worried."

"You got back," I said weakly.

He seemed puzzled; then understanding dawned. "From Kiel? Oh, yes."

The pale evening sun drifted in between the half-drawn curtains. Outside, the trees were black against a copper-colored sky. "What time is it?" I asked him.

He glanced at his wristwatch. "Eight o'clock." He smiled down at me. "Eight o'clock, Monday."

I frowned up at him, trying to take it in. "Monday?"

"That's right. You've been out like a light for some considerable time."

The door opened and my father looked in. When he saw my head turn on the pillow, he was across the room in an instant. "Kathie, my dear, you had us all very worried. How do you feel?"

"Tired," I said. "Very, very tired. What's been wrong with me?"

"High temperature—some kind of fever."

In retrospect, I can see that I had simply not been able to take any more. I'd been through too much in too little time. And the dreadful shock of Richie's death, the final meeting out there on the sands, had been the last straw.

My mind had tried to hang on, but it was the body which had refused.

Johnny stood up. "I'd better be off."

Panic flooded through me instantly and I grabbed for his hand. "Are you on?"

"Good God, no."

I held on to his hand very tightly. "I don't believe you."

"Ask your father. The whole squadron's been stood down."

I turned my head. My father smiled and kissed my hand. "Quite right, Kathie. There isn't a thing to worry about."

"I'm playing for a mess dance, you cuckoo." Johnny looked at his watch. "In exactly half an hour, so I'd better get moving. You have a good night's sleep and I'll see you in the morning."

He kissed me on the forehead and went out. A few minutes later my mother came in with a glass of warm milk and something in it to make me sleep, so that I didn't hear the bombers go out at ten. But I was awake just after dawn when they returned.

So Johnny had been getting on with what had to be done and could not be avoided. The hazards of the calling. My mother had left them shorthanded at the canteen to look after me. And my father, for whom truth was everything, had lied—for my sake.

And what was I doing? Lying flat on my back feeling sorry for myself. It very definitely seemed time I grew up. I flung the bedclothes to one side. I needed to pull myself together, get things working again, and there was one certain way of doing that.

I dressed quickly in sweater and jodhpurs and old riding boots; tiptoed downstairs, aware of movement in the kitchen, and let myself out. Ten minutes later I was galloping Jersey Lil along the dike, the wind in my face, alive again.

When I went in through the side gate I found my father cutting roses. He was still in uniform and glanced up quickly as the latch clicked.

"Kathie?" His face was full of concern. "We were worried about you."

"I know, Daddy." I kissed him. "It was utterly thoughtless of me, but I needed to pull myself together."

He looked at me searchingly. "You're sure you're all right?"

"Never better," I assured him. "No more nonsense. And thanks for what you did for me—last night, I mean."

He said, "Johnny's inside. He arrived about twenty minutes ago."

Strange, but since waking and hearing the Lancasters coming in, I'd taken it completely for granted that he had got back. The very first time I'd known such certainty.

I turned to go. My father said sharply, "Kathie!"

"Yes, Daddy?"

His face was grave. It was as if there were something he wanted to tell me but he couldn't find the right words. He smiled. "Nothing. It's just nice to see you looking your old self again."

As I went up the steps to the terrace, Johnny started to play the Bechstein—that haunting little piece, "Le Pastour," with which Myra Hess had ended her concert. I went in through the French windows and leaned on the end of the piano, watching him. His hair seemed very white in the morning sun. Pale fire. He looked up, that crooked little smile on his mouth.

"Back in the land of the living again. That's good."

"Was it bad last night?"

"Could have been worse. Dortmund. We lost two."

I swallowed hard, hands clenched tightly together as I leaned across the piano. "And tonight? Are you on tonight?"

"So I understand. The boys in the know say Stettin, but that isn't definite. I've got something for you."

He pushed a roll of manuscript across the top of the Bechstein. It was tied with red ribbon, and I opened it out quickly. "The *Rhapsody*. You've finished it?"

He started to play "These Foolish Things." "That's right. I inserted the new section, fair-copied those pages that needed it. All yours now."

"It looks beautiful."

"Richie did most of it, not me."

He spoke that name so calmly. I took a deep breath and pushed it back across the piano. "Play it for me."

He shook his head. "I don't think so."

"Why not?"

"Never again, Kate," he said. "Somebody else, perhaps, but not me."

I stared at him in astonishment and tried again. "Please, Johnny, just for me. After all, this is a special occasion. One to go. What Richie used to call the Big One."

He stopped playing, put a cigarette in his mouth and lit it. "That was yesterday, Kate."

It seemed very, very quiet, and I was somehow cold again. "I don't understand."

"Don't you remember, back in July when I first knew you? Richie came for me here one afternoon when he was short of a mid-upper gunner for an afternoon trip to Kiel?"

"Yes, I remember," I said faintly.

"Which means the Big One was yesterday."

"Ninety," I said. "You mean you've completed ninety? But that can't be! You're on tonight."

"It's simple enough," he said. "Bunny had two in hand

and I always promised I'd see him through. I've spoken to the Winco and he's agreed I can do the extras. They're short on replacements at the moment anyway."

I stood there staring at him dumbly, unable to take it in. "Say something," he said, "if it's only goodbye."

And then I exploded. "You're looking for death!" I shouted. "You're afraid to live!" He put a hand out to touch me. I pulled away. "Why? Give me one good reason!"

"Bunny's in a bad way," he said simply. "He thinks he's for the chop. Can't get over Richie. He needs me."

"*I* need you," I said. "What about *me*?"

"I'm sorry, Kate. That's the way it has to be."

I think at that moment I actually hated him. "Go on!" I screamed. "Get out! Go to your death! Be a hero, but don't think I'll be there to hand out the cups of tea anymore. I've had it." He stood there staring at me, the eyes bleak again. I pushed him in the chest. "Get away from me!"

I leaned on the piano for support. He walked out to the terrace without a word. The MG started up; the engine faded into the distance. There was another step on the terrace. I turned and found my father standing there.

"You knew," I said.

He nodded. "I knew, my dear."

"Why?" I demanded. "I don't understand!"

"He told you. His friend needs him."

"But that's rubbish," I said angrily. "Six JU-88s aren't going to descend on Bunny O'Hara from the clouds just because Johnny isn't in the rear turret. It's superstitious nonsense. Like the way they all used to touch his sleeve for luck. And where did it get them?"

"What do you want from me, Kathie? Another sermon, neatly packaged to answer all your questions?" He shook his head. "That's not reality."

"What is, then?"

He started to fill his pipe. "People, I suppose, and what they are. Not that we ever get to know anybody truly, not even those closest to us. But we can understand partly, like St. Paul." He smiled apologetically. "There I go, speaking like a priest again."

"Are you saying I don't really know Johnny?"

"Something like that."

"And you do?"

"Parts of him. Speaking as a priest again, there was once a man called Martin Luther who said, 'Here I stand. I can do no other.'"

"And you think Johnny is like that?"

"I think that for him, what is the final answer as he sees it becomes the *only* answer possible. He too can do no other. It isn't in his nature." He put a match to the bowl of his pipe and puffed out smoke. "As with this present situation."

I was angry now. Bitterly angry. "What you see as noble and heroic I see as stupid and stubborn. He has no right to do it. It isn't fair!"

"To whom, Kathie? To you?"

Which stopped me in my tracks. I tried to answer him, failed completely and fled from those calm gray eyes to my room.

I went back to bed and stayed there, even refusing the food my mother brought me on a tray. I lay in the gathering darkness writhing in helpless rage as the Lancasters roared over the rectory on their way out to sea. I tossed and turned for most of the night and finally dropped into a troubled sleep in which Richie came to me. He was standing there in flying gear, the spotted scarf fluttering about his neck, the water like black glass between us, that slight ironic smile on his lips.

"Happy ending, kid," he kept saying. "Remember what I told you." And then the green stone spun down through the water in slow motion and bounced off his head. He went over backwards with a cry and floated in front of me, the eyes wide and staring, arms stretching towards me.

I came awake with a start, damp with sweat, to the roaring of engines as the Lancs came home. I lay there for a moment or two only, slightly dazed, and must have drifted off into sleep again, to be awakened by a hand on my shoulder.

It was my mother with a tray. Tea, toast and home-made marmalade and the morning paper. "How do you feel now, dear?"

I pushed myself up against the pillow. "What time is it?"

"Nearly eleven o'clock. I thought I'd leave you. You looked as if you needed it." She put the tray on my knees and moved to the door. There was one question above all that I wanted to ask, but stubborn pride kept me silent. She answered it for me, turning as she opened the door. "It was a bad night, Kathie. They lost five, but Johnny's back."

It took everything I had but I forced the words out. "I couldn't care less."

She showed no emotion whatsoever, simply closed the door and left me alone. I sat there sick and angry with myself as much as with Johnny, and I don't think I've ever felt so miserable. In desperation, I got up, put on my riding clothes and went out.

I stayed on the marsh with Jersey Lil for a good two hours and spent almost an hour brushing and grooming her on my return. It was just after two o'clock when I went back home. My father was sitting on the terrace reading the morning newspaper and drinking tea.

He looked up. "Oh, there you are. The tea's fresh if you're interested, and I brought an extra cup. Just back from running your mother to Upton Magna."

I poured my tea. "What did she want to go up there for?"

"They're shorthanded at the canteen. The usual thing. What have you been doing with yourself?"

"I took Jersey Lil for a long ride on the marshes."

He filled that eternal pipe of his methodically. "Working it off?"

"Working what off?" I demanded.

"Yesterday's anger. I should imagine it's just about turned to self-disgust by now." He struck a match. "I heard most of the things you said to that boy. You were damnably unfair, Kathie." He puffed out smoke and added calmly, "I wonder whether it wouldn't be perhaps honest to admit that much of the anguish, the terror and the pain of the past couple of months you've really seen from your point of view rather than his."

I was genuinely shocked. "That's a horrible thing to say."

"Is it?" He glanced at his watch. "He's leaving for Essen at ten to three. A five-hour trip—am I right?" I could hardly breathe and pushed myself up on to my feet. "The North Sea, Holland, into the heart of Germany," my father said; "then all the way back with every Luftwaffe fighter base alert and waiting. Five hours of hell, Kathie, but who for? Johnny or you?"

There was no answer to that, or at least not one that I was capable of facing. I said, "Please, Daddy, will you take me? Now?"

"Of course, my dear." He stood up and we went down the steps of the terrace together.

We were just too late, for as we turned in through the main gate, the lead Lancaster roared down the runway and lifted off, to be followed by the rest in quick succession. *Dark Rosaleen* was number four; I saw her flash by as we drove up to the dispersal area and braked to a halt beside the canteen.

I jumped out, and as my father joined me I said, "I'm too late, Daddy."

"Wait here," he said. "I'll see what I can do."

He hurried away towards the tower, and my mother appeared at my side. "Come and sit down. A cup of tea will work wonders."

I did as I was told, mainly because I was too weary, too utterly dejected to do anything else. I found myself sitting on the bunk at the rear of the caravan, balancing a cup of tea on my knees—the bunk on which the truck driver had died on that terrible day the Germans attacked the airfield.

Had it really happened? Any of it? For a moment, my nostrils were filled with the stench of burning flesh again. I shuddered, and then the door opened and my father looked in.

"Ah, there you are. They proved sympathetic enough in control to send this message for you."

He passed me a signal flimsy. It simply said: *Sorry I missed you. Here when you get back.*

"Was it acknowledged?" I asked.

"Oh, yes."

He passed me another flimsy. This one read: *Get the piano tuned.* I looked up at my father, too full for words. He said, "It's going to be all right, Kathie. Just believe that and don't let go."

He went out and I lay back on the bunk, eyes closed, and clutched the signal flimsy to me.

12

IT WAS A LONG AFTERNOON. When the news started to filter down from control towards evening, it was all bad, for the Lancasters had taken the same kind of battering the American Flying Fortresses had undergone in one ferocious daylight raid after another for months now. The Group, as a whole, lost thirty-seven. Johnny's squadron, two on the way to Dortmund, two over the target and one more on the way back over Holland.

The rest were badly mauled, the first planes to touch down showing every evidence of the punishment they had taken. I stood by the the caravan with my father, looking up through his field glasses for *Dark Rosaleen*, but there was no sign.

"Come on, Bunny, come on!" I whispered desperately.

The crews of the first planes to land were making their way to the canteen now, and the hell that this one had been showed on their faces. We waited. There was an emergency landing at one point, the kite plowing off one of the secondary runways on its belly. The ambulances were finding plenty to do.

Nothing seemed to be happening. Some of the crews

started to move off to debriefing. Someone shouted, "What's this?"

A Lancaster limped in from the sea at fifteen hundred. Smoke poured from the port outer, and the starboard outer was feathered. It was *Dark Rosaleen*; I knew it even before I got the glasses focused and saw the damaged tail plane.

She circled above the airfield, and a black bundle erupted beneath her that was a man clutching his knees, turning over and over. White silk flared as a parachute opened. And then another.

The men about me fell silent as the parachutists descended. Someone said softly, "What's going on, for Christ's sake?"

The first parachutist landed on the far side of the main runway, and as a jeep raced forward, the other came down fifty yards further on. An ambulance turned towards him, and my father said, "I'll go up to the tower. See what I can find out."

Dark Rosaleen circled lazily, dropping a little lower with every passing moment. The jeep came back to dispersal with the first parachutist. It was the navigator, a boy called Tony Pierce. Everyone crowded round.

It was my mother who called, "Give him a chance to breathe" and pushed her way through the crowd with a cup of tea.

Pierce drank gratefully. "It's a shambles up there. The bomb aimer was killed by flak over the target, and we were plastered by fighters on the way back. Had four ME-109s on our tail from Den Helder and halfway across the pond."

"What's going on?" somebody demanded.

"The inside of the kite's a mess. Most of the chutes are U/S, and Higgins, the flight engineer, and Jacky Dawson, the wireless op, are both badly shot up. Bunny told

Rogers and me to jump. He's going to try for a landing later when he's used up some more juice. The tanks are leaking like a sieve."

I plucked at his sleeve. "What about Johnny?"

He swallowed hard, trying to find words. "Stayed to help him. Bunny took shrapnel in his left hand and leg."

So that was that. The final nightmare was now reality. I stayed where I was—ignoring the stares, the whispers; watching through the glasses. After a while, my father appeared. "Have you heard?"

I nodded. "What are their chances?"

"Not good. The undercarriage is damaged, so it will have to be a belly landing. It's those leaking tanks O'Hara is worried about. Not too good for that kind of landing, and he's weakening himself, it seems."

"And Johnny?"

"He's fine. His chute is still intact. O'Hara ordered him to get out, but he refused."

They were under a thousand feet now. I didn't know what to say, and yet this time there was no numbness, no withdrawal. I raised the glasses and said desperately, "Johnny Stewart, if you die on me now I'll never forgive you."

I almost expected to see his face, the crooked smile as if he enjoyed the joke—and then everything happened at once as black smoke gushed from the port inner.

Bunny must have acted instinctively. He went down fast, banked to starboard over the far end of the airfield and brought her in. It must have taken both of them to hold the stick, and they almost made it. In the final moment, the port wing dipped, striking sparks from the runway. *Dark Rosaleen* skidded sideways, then plowed on in an enormous slide that seemed as if it would never end, flames flickering along the port wing. She ground to a halt in a cloud of dust, smoke billowing up.

The fire tenders and ambulances were already racing along the perimeter. I found myself running, aware of my father's voice raised in alarm, others calling me back. But nothing could have stopped me then.

Black smoke swirled around me. I could hear the sirens of the fire tenders, the crackling of flames, and thought of those leaking tanks with horror. And then, a sudden gust of wind tore a hole in the smoke and I saw two figures in flying jackets stumbling towards me not twenty yards away. *Johnny and Bunny O'Hara.*

Behind them, men swarmed all over *Dark Rosaleen*, extinguishing the flames, and already the first of the wounded was being passed out through the hatch. Bunny slid to the ground and sat clutching his left leg, laughing inanely. Johnny stood there swaying, face blackened by the smoke, then took a hesitant step forward and called my name.

I ran into his arms. It was over.

EPILOGUE

From the terrace in the evening light, I can see him now, working amongst the roses. Older, of course; a little stiffer with the years. Yet when he lifts his head and looks towards me, it might still be the same fair-haired boy I met in the church on that distant summer's evening so many years ago. Richie, dear Richie, was right, you see. Some stories do have happy endings, even in real life. . . .

81-118

F   Patterson, Sarah
Pat   The distant summer.

DATE DUE

MAY 12 1981		
AUG 01 1981		
NOV 05 1981		
JUL 22 '86		
JAN 30 1987		